To Everett,\
Best wishes\
1 Gerald

WRUSH

by The Karakul

The Secret Worlds
of Tabetha Bright

VOLUME ONE

BY THE KARAKUL

EMERALD
BOOK CO.

Published by Emerald Book Company
Austin, TX
www.emeraldbookcompany.com

For ordering information, please visit www.TheSecretWorlds.com
Design and composition by Greenleaf Book Group
Illustration and cover design by Ruke (www.RukeStudios.com)

Publisher's Cataloging-In-Publication Data
(Prepared by The Donohue Group, Inc.)

Karakul.
    Wrush / by the Karakul. -- 1st ed.

    p. ; cm. -- (The secret worlds of Tabetha Bright ; v. 1)

        Summary: A young girl who is confined to a wheelchair receives a magical pen and is able to draw herself into the enchanted world of Wrush where she will become the empress. A magical adventure ensues.
    ISBN: 978-1-934572-38-2

    1. Children with disabilities--Juvenile fiction. 2. Empresses--Juvenile fiction. 3. Children with disabilities--Fiction. 4. Empresses--Fiction. 5. Fantasy. 6. Fantasy fiction. I. Title.

PZ7.K127 Wr 2010   2010922233
[Fic]

Part of the Tree Neutral™ program, which offsets the number of trees consumed in the production and printing of this book by taking proactive steps, such as planting trees in direct proportion to the number of trees used: www.treeneutral.com

TreeNeutral®

Printed in Canada on acid-free paper
10 11 12 13 14 15   10 9 8 7 6 5 4
First Edition

To Anika,
for whom every pen is magic . . .

Part One

Author's Note

You may ask, why such secrecy? Why hide this story from view? It may seem strange at first that I've kept it buried so long, until you understand one thing: This tale was never meant to be told. It came to me from an old man who claims he played some small part as a boy and asked only that I keep this story hidden. From what, or whom, I was never told, and for many years I have lain awake and wondered.

Until now.

Now I myself am old, grey, and gnarled as an oak. The days left to me are few, and if there is one thing more precious to an old man than secrets, it is time. Yes, time. And the time for this story's telling has come. What I'm about to tell you may seem too extraordinary to believe. Whether you choose to is beyond my care. It is written here within these pages, which I have bound with yellow twine.

My name is The Karakul.

Her heart thundered as she wrote the first line.

*I*t has been said that stars, even our own dear sun in the sky, burn at their brightest just before they die out. In a mighty explosion of light they grow to many times their own size, swallowing darkness and even the planets about them. Then in the blink of an eye, between the beats of a heart, they are gone. The star is quenched like a candle's wick in the breeze.

I tell you this not simply out of interest, but because such a thing happened once on Earth. Only it was not a star that filled the darkness. It was a girl. And that mightiest light was something in her eyes.

This is the story of Tabetha Bright, an ordinary child who was to be responsible for a most extraordinary event. I would speak of this event now, for it is so astounding in itself, but I fear you would not appreciate the greatness of that day—the day Tabetha changed the world—unless I start at the very beginning.

And it began with whispering.

Whispering in the hall. Tabetha Bright sat up in her small, dreary bed in the corner of her small, dreary room in the corner of the dreariest old hospital one can imagine. She heard her mother and the doctor speaking in hushed tones. Whenever they whispered like this, Tabetha felt a spark of fear jump within her. She had been ill a very long time, and lately there was more whispering than ever.

"But she'll be heartbroken!" her mother hissed. Tabetha saw them now, her mother and the doctor, arguing quietly in the corridor beyond her door. Her mother's hands fluttered about like a pair of angry birds, landing first on her hips, then balled under her arms, then back on her hips, fiercely tapping. "It's Tabetha's birthday! You can't ask her to stay. I already promised to take her home!"

"It's not about her birthday—" the doctor started to say, but Tabetha's mother cut him off. "What if we have her back by tonight? Or even earlier, like this afternoon?"

Now, dear reader, it is entirely possible that Tabetha, in all her short life, had never looked forward to a single day with more feeling. She was in a fever of anticipation. Her little heart tapped in her chest and all her attention, as if straining to hear a faint voice on the wind, was stretched around the doctor's silence in the hall.

Maybe, maybe, maybe, maybe, she mouthed from her bed, knowing that when an adult says *maybe,* you're doing pretty well. Because *maybe* usually means *probably.* And *probably* is pretty close to yes. But for some reason, adults prefer to start with—

"No." The doctor shook his head and Tabetha slumped inside. She felt her heart sink down into her belly.

"Mrs. Bright," he began, his voice pained and slow, "your daughter is not a very healthy girl. To be perfectly honest, we don't even know exactly what's wrong. Now, I know she appears happy, and she gets around fine in her wheelchair, but you have to accept that Tabetha's not like other children."

Which Tabetha knew. How could she forget, lying there in her bed, staring at the same boring walls day after day? She knew having something called *pneumonia* now made things even worse, and she knew her parents couldn't afford the medicine. And she knew the medicine came free, every day at noon, so long as she stayed here in the hospital.

Reluctantly, Tabetha perked up her ears. She caught something about *still running some tests* . . . and *once we know what we're dealing with* . . . Then: "You've seen it yourself, Mrs. Bright. She's fragile. And with pneumonia on top of it all, quite frankly, anything could happen." In an even lower voice the doctor repeated, "Anything . . ."

Tabetha's mother crossed and uncrossed her arms. She looked away and touched her eye.

With one finger, the doctor slowly pushed his glasses higher on his nose. He cleared his throat, then delivered the classic finish: "I know it's hard, Mrs. Bright, but I really think this is the best place for your daughter right now."

I will not lie to you, reader. I will not speak of miraculous cures. I will not describe a rescue that in fact never took place. On the contrary. I tell you now, Tabetha did not go home on this day or any other till the end when each of us goes home in our own way. But there is no misfortune here. Sorrow is but the yardstick of joy. And as you shall soon see, no greater birthday has ever come to pass.

Tabetha puffed the hair from her eyes and took up her pens and paper. Morning light dazzled the film of dust on her window. It was warm in the sun and she was eight years old today and she made the very clear decision to be glad. Her legs might be thin and limp as wet noodles, and her chest might ache when she breathed, but so long as she had pens and paper, Tabetha could enjoy the one thing she loved most:

Writing.

Tabetha could write stories all day long and stay up half the night putting pictures to her words and never once think of food, or sleep, or television, or friends, or anything else outside her secret world. Writing took Tabetha to that place inside where magic was real and alive.

With pen tip flying, Tabetha dove into the story she'd begun earlier that morning, part of a mystery series involving some unusual characters—an electric chicken, a talking cookie, a pair of tigers playing chess—setting each completed page into a stack on her wheelchair.

Out in the corridor, the dry click of whispers droned on and on, then halted in a way that made silence roar. "I'm . . . I'm sorry," the doctor muttered under his breath and Tabetha heard her mother's muffled tears.

She set down her pen and called from her bed, "You don't need to cry, Mom! I'll be okay here tonight!" It frightened Tabetha when her mother cried. "I'll see you again when you come back tomorrow!"

Her mother smiled back through the tears, but her smile was too big. Adults did that when a smile wasn't for real. She blew Tabetha a sad-happy kiss, then spoke again with the doctor while Tabetha wrote about Dream Melons and Mole Dragons and Tree Squid smoking pipes. Then, without even meaning to, while doodling in the margins, Tabetha discovered she had drawn the pale lovely face of an empress.

An empress, I might add here, that looked very much like herself.

Of course, the empress wore a crown and perhaps the wavy hair was a bit longer, but the Disney-brown eyes, I assure you, were pure Tabetha. She sort of chuckled to herself, thinking what a strange thing to do, drawing a picture of herself without even knowing. Then she tried to imagine an empress in a wheelchair and the smile fled from her face. *And probably no empress ever lived alone in a hospital.*

Tabetha spent the next minute in a kind of soft sadness, thinking of all those things normal children could do. Then she noticed the sunlight again and recalled her decision to be glad. Her only wish now was to share it.

If only I had a brother, Tabetha thought. She had always wanted a brother. An older one, supposing elder siblings made the world a bit safer. After a moment's thought she picked up her pen and added one more person to the story: a boy, not at all like herself, but someone she needed to include nonetheless.

After her mother left, Tabetha scooped her pens and coloring pencils from the wrinkled sheets and wrapped them tightly with a rubber band. It was quiet in her room, and she felt quiet too. She heard a fly bouncing against the window. A nurse laughing in the hall. Her legs were starting to ache, which meant the morning was getting on.

She tucked her many pages into a neat stack, tapping the edges, and then leaned across her bed. She was about to set them with the others, in the seat of her wheelchair, when she noticed a small box waiting there. It sat atop her story. She picked it up.

"Where did this come from?" She looked around the room, but was as alone as ever. The box seemed to have simply appeared.

It was a pen box, which meant it was quite small, but something about it gave the impression of size; as if cities, mountains, long roaring plains, all of it had been pressed under its lid. Tabetha tested its weight in one hand. It felt heavy. Which was strange, as she knew for certain it weighed almost nothing at all. The box was wooden and polished, and the grain swirled and shone. Stuck to the lid was a tiny note, about the size of a stamp. On closer inspection, she saw that it *was* a stamp, as though the box had been sent from somewhere far away, except that written upon it, in elegant blue script, was this:

To Tabetha
From Wrush
Have a fantastic birthday!

Tabetha carefully pulled the stamp from the box, studying the tiny words through a squint. Who in the world was Wrush? And how did someone deliver this box without Tabetha noticing?

A tingly sensation crept up her spine.

Tabetha quickly pressed the stamp back onto the box. She placed her thumbs on the box's edge, preparing to flip open the lid, when she noticed her reflection in the polished surface of the wood. Her face shone back, and she could see the mirror image of her thumbs. But everything in the room behind her was different. It was as though another room was reflected, one she had never been to or seen. She watched her own eyes grow big as coins.

Leaning closer, she could make out the details of thrones behind her. She saw seven of them, all in a line, against the back wall of an enormous chamber in a palace. The image was so clear, Tabetha almost felt herself tumbling in. She startled, and blinked away the strange image.

"Now that was weird," she muttered to herself—just as her thumbs, under no guidance of her own, flipped open the hinged lid with a *click*.

Inside was a pen. It lay, as though sleeping, in the soft molds of blue felt. The pen was made of wood, just like the box. Tabetha touched first the blue felt, then the length of the pen, stroking it with slow, wondrous care.

She stared, unable to pull her eyes from the sight. What followed, she would later say, was perhaps the first important moment of her life.

In an excited rush, she reached across her bed and snatched a fresh sheet of paper from the seat of her wheelchair. She fingered the pen from its box, thumb-clicked the top, and the narrow tip appeared. She held it up before her, and her muscles froze.

"Whoooaa . . . ," she cooed, the hair prickling the back of her neck. The pen's tip began glowing like a coal. She watched colors, soft as smoke, curling up from the pen: a writhing cloud of oily rainbows. A chill gently shook her, both delicious and eerie. The pen grew warm in her hand, and she felt the first spark of alarm.

Figures were taking shape in the mist.

There were faces. Creatures. Stars and planets. A whole world was congealing in the fog. Tabetha watched herds of cloud-animals go tromping through a sky where the sun burned purple and blue. There was lightning over temples, a smell like darkness catching fire, explosions of violet powder packed with feeling.

Then, without warning, all the oily rainbows and their swirling world hues were sucked back into the pen's black tip.

Tabetha felt the corners of her mouth pulling into a grin. A warm excitement fluttered in her belly. Staring at the magic pen in her hand, she lowered its tip to the page in her lap.

Her heart thundered as she wrote the first line.

"I'll hide you myself."

There was a crack to the air and Tabetha jolted, nearly dropping the pen in her lap. She glanced down at the page and gasped, "The ink is alive!" The single line she had written now squirmed across the page like an electric eel.

She wrote a second line. The ink shimmered and rippled like lights across water. It made her stomach feel woozy just to watch it. In a flurry of excitement, Tabetha scribbled out one word, in enormous letters across the center of the page:

FIRE

She studied the word a moment, then very carefully reached down and touched it with the end of her finger.

"Ouch!" she yelped. "It's hot!

For the next hour, Tabetha Bright forgot about everything in this world. She was so busy writing her story, she forgot all about her wheelchair and her loneliness, about her mother's tears when she left. She forgot about her pneumonia and the dull ache in her legs. Tabetha wrote more skillfully than ever before, and when she finished, she read the story through, from beginning to end.

"My best one yet," she decided at once. Tabetha couldn't believe how realistic it seemed. Studying the words, she found her eyes went funny, no longer able to see the ink. Instead they peered *right through it,* gazing into the steady eyes of a gorilla with biceps like black pumpkins and big, bushy eyebrows and a forehead that sloped back to a crest. He hung in a tree so real Tabetha nearly believed she could reach straight into the page and join him.

If my legs could actually work, that is. The thought crashed in like a ball through the window, her shattered hopes made twinkling and sharp. It was funny, sometimes you could actually forget you were ill. Sometimes everything seemed normal until you tried to stand. And then you remembered, because that was the thing about difficulty: Forgetting it doesn't make it go away.

With a sigh, she folded the magic story in half. Then in half again. She touched it lightly on the corner and slid it beneath her pillow. She felt good, warm inside. It had been quite a morning, and she rarely made it this long without a nap. She set the pen back in its box. She lay back in her bed and curled into her sheets. Before she knew it, Tabetha was fast asleep.

She knew she was dreaming.

She knew because she could walk, and she hadn't walked since she was four. Tabetha wandered across the field that stretched behind her old house, the sky above her an impossible blue. It was quiet, sparkling. No one was around.

She ran through mixed grasses so tall they slapped at her chest, her eyes fixed on the hill beyond the fence-line. It swelled lonely and grand, carpeted in tiny blue flowers. Forget-me-nots, she thought they were called. The flowers grew so thick that from a distance they were one, the hill like a giant, half-buried plum.

She climbed it, feeling the sun on her cheeks. She lay down upon the summit and wept. It was always like this—blue flowers, blue sky. Tears without sadness. And she was not alone. And this hill was her home. Only when she shut her eyes did she wake.

Tabetha stirred from her dream, a strange dream. She'd had it before and each time it was the same: her eyes fluttering open, a blurred moment of confusion, and then a rich jumble of feelings thick as cream in her chest. What was that blue hill all about? Even now, with the images still fresh, she had no idea why this dream kept returning.

Tabetha rolled to her side, only to find the corner of her story poking out from beneath the pillow. Drowsily, she pulled it free, recalling first the sadness, then the sudden enchantment of her morning with the pen.

Tabetha unfolded the paper. She blinked, flipping the page over, and then back again to be sure. The page was blank! There was nothing there, not a single mark!

It was then that Tabetha first noticed something very unusual about her hospital room. Her eyes drifted from one wall to the next, her mouth forming a silent *Oh.*

She had never seen so many beautiful plants crowded into a single space. Not just bouquets from the flower store, but heaps of plants everywhere. Her room bulged like a jungle greenhouse. There were tropical trees and vines twisting up the wall, mosses so green she could smell them. Tabetha wondered briefly if a child, given the hazy and sometimes confusing borders of the imagination, ever knew for certain when she had woken from a dream. Until something soft slapped her wrist. Something soft and yellow.

Tabetha glanced down, her whole face pinched with bewilderment. She turned the object over in her hand. A *banana peel?* She even smelled it to be sure. But what was a banana peel doing in her bedroom? And who had been rude enough to throw such a thing?

With a tiny yelp, Tabetha's breath caught in her throat. Her heart pounded like a gong. Slowly, she brushed the hair from her eyes, staring intently past the foot of her bed where something humongous and black and hairy was noisily munching away at an armful of bananas.

It was a gorilla.

It was a very big gorilla, and Tabetha breathed sharply as he leaped onto her bed. He gazed straight into her eyes, three-toed-sloth-calm.

"Wow," she whispered slowly, her pulse knocking in her ears, for she had, so far as she could tell, just *written* a gorilla to life. She sat stone-still, her gaze wide and unblinking, making certain, absolutely certain this was real.

It was, she decided. It was very much real. She considered whether this might pose a problem.

"Well, are you a . . . are you a friendly sort of gorilla?"

He said nothing, of course, just stuffed bananas into the black pouch of each cheek, chewing thoughtfully and slowly (with mouth closed, she noticed) and all the while watching Tabetha with those sloth-calm eyes. He sure seemed friendly enough. Tabetha was lonely. And hospital rules were rather vague on the point of African primates. But somewhere deep down, Tabetha knew he had to go.

"Well, you seem like a pretty nice guy," she explained to him. "But Pizza, that's my dog, he isn't even allowed in here to visit. So you can imagine the trouble I'll be in if the nurses find you."

The gorilla just stared at her, chewing.

Tabetha cleared her throat. "So. You'll have to go now."

Staring. Chewing.

"Okay," she said. "I'll put it another way. Wherever your home is? That's where you need to go. Away. Do you understand?"

He stopped chewing.

Picked his nose.

Began chewing again.

"Forget it," she said, shaking her head. "I'll hide you myself."

Tabetha glanced around her room, taking in the fig trees and bromeliads. A lizard skittered up the vines on her wall.

Hiding all this, it suddenly occurred to her, would not be like spitting something back into her napkin. What she needed was a plan.

"I've got it!" She snapped her fingers. "You stay put," she said to the gorilla. "I may not be big enough or strong enough to hide you. But maybe I can bring in someone who is."

Tabetha seized a fresh sheet of paper. She flipped open her pen box and yanked out the magic pen. *Why didn't I think of this before?* she asked herself, inwardly chuckling at her own genius, and with the scratch of pen against paper she began to describe the one creature that was sure to change her luck.

"A giant," she murmured aloud.

And nothing would ever be the same again.

*I*ndeed, I expect you, as a reader, may have noticed a small flaw in Tabetha's thinking. "A slight miscalculation," you might tell your friends. "She made a wee mistake." You might even think you could have done better.

You are wrong.

Let me assure you, it is one thing to be *reading* about gorillas, safe and sound in your bed, and quite another to have one rumpling the covers; and it is a known fact that the heart is most brave when furthest from danger. So! Abandon your pride for the moment, your lazy conceit. It is necessary that you understand this: Tabetha Bright was an extremely clever young girl.

Perhaps she was more young than clever at this point in the story, but very soon now all that will change. You will see. Like starting a fire in a storm, cleverness does not catch all at once.

Tabetha's would take a few more strikes of the match. Yet by the end of this tale, you may need to shield your eyes, for you will find not a girl but a blaze.

Tabetha finished her description and read it over with care, making sure the giant appeared friendly enough to help hide the gorilla. Then she folded the paper in half, just like before.

"One . . . two . . . three," she counted. She slowly unfolded the paper.

"It worked!" she cheered aloud. The sheet of paper was blank! And if the giant wasn't on the paper anymore, that meant—

Boom!

Tabetha dropped the paper.

Boom! Boom!

She grabbed hold of the sheets.

Boom! Boom! CRASH!

Her whole bed bounced, and then jerked around as if in an earthquake as something large, very large, shoved up from beneath. Tabetha shrieked. Two huge hands emerged, one on either side of her bed, and Tabetha tugged the covers up to her neck. She saw the zucchini-fat fingers, the dirt under their nails. They curled around the side-rails of her bed and then hoisted it into the air. Tabetha and the gorilla tipped side to side like a boat between the crests of two waves.

A giant climbed out from underneath.

"Goodness!" he boomed, his voice shaking flakes from the ceiling. He appeared surprised to find Tabetha, sitting speechless atop her bed, a terrified girl in blue pajamas. He quickly set her bed back on the floor.

"Well, now this is unexpected," he said, scratching his thick jaw. "One minute I'm strolling through the woods, searching for my cat, and next thing I know, I'm here." He stopped suddenly, lifting a suspicious brow in Tabetha's direction. "You're not an *elf*, are you?"

Tabetha shook her head.

"Good," he said. "Good for us both, I think. Far too much mischief in an elf, and you've got an honest face, if I had to guess. And you're certainly not a Gwybie or I'd smell you from here. So what sort of creature are you then?"

Tabetha stared up at the giant, who was so enormous his head was hunched low, his back and shoulders pressed tight against the ceiling. His nose was big as a tree stump, and his hair was shaggy and brown. His eyes, which twinkled and blinked, were the color of calm water at night.

"I'm a girl," she said. "I'm eight."

"A girl! All alone in these woods? Have you any idea of the danger?"

Tabetha glanced around. "This is my room," she said. "It's a hospital. You're in my room now because I wrote about you."

She showed the giant her pen, and he nodded slowly in understanding.

"Ahhh," he grunted. "A magic pen. So that explains it. Well, if you'll excuse me then, I best be going. Got to keep searching for Elsewhere."

"Elsewhere?"

"My cat," said the giant. "Elsewhere's his name. Not that he'll come when you call him."

"Maybe if he had a different name," suggested Tabetha.

"*Maybe* if I just left him behind for once!" said the giant, obviously frustrated. "That would teach him a lesson. Serve him right, too. Make a cat think twice before misplacing himself."

"You can't leave him!" said Tabetha, who was mostly fond of small animals. "Besides," she said. "I can help you find your cat. And you can help me too."

After a pause, the giant agreed that this was reasonable. He listened to Tabetha explain her concern.

"Well you see," she began, "I have this gorilla on my bed. Twice now I've asked him to go, but he just sits there."

The giant tapped his chin; his eyes narrowed in thought. "Yes, I see what you mean. But are you sure this is actually a problem?"

"Pretty sure."

"Hmmm," the giant rumbled, tapping his chin one last time. "Perhaps he's just lost," he suggested. "Like me."

"He's not lost. He's just not where he belongs. And I really need him hidden before the nurses come."

"Then there's definitely a problem," grumbled the giant, looking from the gorilla to the door. "Because if I can't fit through your doorway, how am I supposed to get him out?"

Tabetha frowned, chewing her lip. This pen, for all the excitement of it, was turning into quite a responsibility. For the first time, she pondered where all this was going.

The giant too was deep in thought. He studied his tremendous hands, flexing them into fists the size of tractor tires. "I suppose I could smash out a bigger doorway."

Tabetha shook her head. "Far too messy. The nurses would probably notice."

"And if I just lifted the ceiling a bit?"

"Then the rain would get in." *Seriously,* thought Tabetha, *some people just don't think things through.*

Suddenly footsteps echoed in the hallway beyond her door. "It's them now!" she whispered. "The nurses! They check on me all the time. Quick, you have to hide!"

"Hide?" He frowned around the room. "I am a giant, remember? If I could hide, there would be no problem in the first place." All the same, he did his best to blend in with the plants. The gorilla, however, sat steady as a stump at the end of her bed.

The clicking of shoes grew louder in the hall. The nurse was getting closer.

"Go!" Tabetha hissed at the gorilla, flapping her arms in a panic. "Git! You've got to hide!"

The gorilla watched her, chewing, calm as ever, showing no sign of the swiftness that must carry him through trees. Then he swallowed, burped loudly, and to Tabetha's dismay, stuck out his tongue and blew a raspberry.

Tabetha sighed. She was finally forced to admit she was on her own. Any smart ideas would have to be hers. Without a second to lose, she grabbed another sheet of paper, picked up her magic pen and scribbled a quick line about the gorilla and the giant. But this time she put them in disguise, describing them both into bright red princess gowns.

A nurse stepped into the room.

"Saints alive!" she declared at once. "Why's it always so darn dark in here?" And Tabetha breathed a sigh of relief, for it was none other than Nurse Myrtle, who was probably about two hundred years old.

Nurse Myrtle had always reminded Tabetha of Yoda in a cardigan, the way she scuttled about the halls with a cane in each fist, swatting away those patients who offered a hand. She weighed about sixty pounds with her jewelry on. Her eyesight was little better than a potato's. Tabetha usually encountered her squinting into rooms, as though peering through a crack in the wall, flicking at light switches that were already on.

"That's better!" Nurse Myrtle announced, swinging her famous flashlight about the well-lit interior of Tabetha's room. "Now goodness me, what have we here? I don't believe I've ever seen so many plants in one patient's room. And what's this!" Nurse Myrtle stopped beside the bed, squinting up at the gorilla and the giant in their frilly red dresses.

Tabetha took a deep breath and held it.

Nurse Myrtle stared.

She frowned.

She worked the dentures around in her mouth.

"Tabetha, my dear," she said at long last, the baggy skin of her neck wobbling like Jello. "I did not realize you had visitors."

Tabetha heard the faint squeak of her own breath as it left her in a rush.

"Rather fashionable ones, too," Nurse Myrtle added with gusto. "Forgive me, my girl. I nearly forgot it was your birthday.

I'll come back later when your guests have gone. Taking your temperature is nothing too urgent."

"That would be great," said Tabetha. "My friends won't be long. I promise. And help yourself to a banana on the way out."

Nurse Myrtle peered closely at Tabetha's guests one last time, and then tugged a ripe banana from the gorilla's arms before leaving.

"That was way too close," Tabetha huffed after Nurse Myrtle had gone. "I need to fix this mess before it gets any worse."

She glanced about. The gorilla had begun ripping limbs down from the small trees to build himself a sleeping nest. The giant, big as he was, had a brain the size of a booger. Yup, she was definitely on her own here. Tabetha smoothed the covers of her bed, brushing a few black hairs to the floor.

A thought came to her. "You said something before," she reminded the giant. "You said something about being lost. And about strolling through woods. Where exactly are you from, anyway?"

The giant grinned, but it was not the normal sort of grin. No, this was the slow, lip-biting, contagious sort of grin that sneaks across a face when you've guessed a secret.

"I was wondering when you'd ask," the giant said in a voice that made her tingle, and Tabetha froze.

Things were not as they seemed. In that instant, as she gazed into his suddenly wise, twinkling eyes, it seemed he knew more, lots more, than the lumbering giant with tractor-tire fists. He wasn't lost, she realized. Nor was he stuck. He wasn't dumb or dim; perhaps he wasn't even looking for a cat. If this giant, with his mysterious grin, was anything at all, he was *waiting* . . . waiting for Tabetha to figure all this out on her own.

She picked up the pen box. She read the words on the stamp. *To Tabetha*, it said. *From Wrush*. Which made no sense, no matter how she worked it in her mind. Who was this Wrush? How did he know who she was? She read the words a last time, and suddenly it came to her. All at once.

"Wrush isn't a person, is it," she said, and the giant shook his head, looking her straight in the eye.

"It's a place," she said. "It's a world. Wrush is where you come from, both you and the gorilla, and I brought you here with my pen."

The giant nodded.

"Wrush," she whispered to herself, touching the words on the stamp. A whole other world . . .

"What's it like there?" she asked. "Are there other children, like me?"

The giant's grin deepened. "See for yourself."

Tabetha realized she held the pen in her hand.

A stack of paper rested in her lap.

Without understanding, without hesitation or thought, Tabetha began to write. One page after another, she wrote and she wrote until the words took on a pulse of their own. She wrote stories about Munglings and Gwybies and three-headed Thworks. She wrote about Sleep Storms sweeping down through the hills.

There was another world out there, so close she could taste it, and each sentence she wrote pulled it nearer. Tabetha wrote until the sun went down, and still she hunched over her story. She wrote until the mushrooms grew tall in the forest around her and the wind and the rain tousled her hair . . .

When at last Tabetha finished, and her many pages lay scattered like a paper skirt about her waist, Tabetha Bright put down her pen. And looked up.

And nothing would ever be the same again.

"Now that is the question!"

Have you, my dear reader, ever dreamed of the impossible? Of enchanted worlds locked away, or hidden in the creases of your own? Dream no more. Such a world is upon you. Read further if you do not yet understand.

The walls of Tabetha's room were gone, vanished. Her curtains were now the green leaves of a forest. The moon and the stars shone through where her ceiling had been, and a warm breeze brushed her cheek, shaking rainwater from the treetops high above. The only thing that remained of the hospital Tabetha once knew was her bed. She threw back the covers in amazement.

"Giant?" she called out. "Gorilla? Is anyone there?"

Only the sounds of a rainforest replied. Her new friends were gone, and Tabetha was alone in a land very different from anywhere she had ever been.

"Where am I?" she said as a glistening moth, big as a pigeon, flopped through the moonlight to perch on her bed. She held out two fingers and it climbed on, her hand dipping to catch its weight.

She set the moth in her lap, its wings pumping lazily as it inspected the faded blue of her pajamas. She thought, *Some days are like that.* Some days just picked you right up and put you back down and the ground beneath you had changed. Tabetha glanced around the forest in wonder. "Did my magic pen do all this?" she murmured aloud.

"Now that is the question!" came a voice through the woods. Tabetha's head popped up at the sound. "Oh yes, the question indeed. Was it the magic pen that made all this? Or did *all this* make the magic pen?" Tabetha turned her head just in time to see the leaves of the forest part and a puffy little face peer out from between them.

"Ah! There you are!" said the creature to Tabetha as he pushed himself free of the foliage. Instead of introducing himself, the creature simply climbed into Tabetha's lap.

The sight of him was so startling and odd that Tabetha could only smile. She studied him from head to tail. When he sat up tall, she realized, he was even bigger than herself, and chubby as a grub, with six arms or legs—though she couldn't be sure. To Tabetha, he looked just like a caterpillar made from bits of the sun, and when he scuttled around, he glowed.

"You," he announced, "must be the one."

"The one?"

"The little girl come to save us all."

"Me?" said Tabetha, wrinkling her nose in confusion. "Save you? I think you've made a mistake. I can't help anyone. I'm just a little girl, and I'm not even completely sure where I am."

"Then let me welcome you," said the funny little creature, "for you are now in the most wonderful empire of Wrush." The creature bowed deeply, throwing back four of his arms with a flourish. "Many have dreamed, and there are those who've had glimpses, but very few children, in fact, ever find their way here. Consider yourself among the lucky."

"I've never been lucky before."

"Ahh!" he said. "All things change now!"

"Everything?" she asked.

"Everything!" He smiled. "And always. The trick is in not getting left behind, but I think you know that already. You're not like the others. I sense it. You're different from those children who have come before."

Tabetha glanced around her. "But I don't know what you're talking about. All I did was write a stor—wow!" she said as the creature wiggled close and began flashing in colors she'd never seen. He felt squishy against her skin and smelled fresh as the top of a baby's head. Tabetha poked at his soft belly and watched the colors pulse at her touch. "You're so . . . electric!" she exclaimed. "What sort of creature are you, anyway?"

"I'm a Mungling," he answered. "The only one in the empire. I've been sent to find you and bring you back to Etherios, the floating capital of Wrush."

Tabetha pushed back from him. "You were expecting me? But that's not possible."

"Everything is possible in the empire of Wrush," the Mungling said. "And everyone in Etherios is eager to meet with their new empress."

An empress! Tabetha had to admit, going to see an empress in a floating city would be the perfect way to spend her birthday. "If I come with you, could I meet the empress too?"

"Meet her!" The Mungling clapped his many hands with amusement. "Little Tabetha, you might even *be* her!" He leaned in so close, she felt the soft heat of his glow. "But there's only one way to find out for sure."

ℛ_l

The Mungling began sniffing at Tabetha's pajama pockets. Then her slippers. He tapped the face of her watch. When he began sniffing her hair, she flinched. "What are you doing? That tickles!"

The Mungling took a deep breath and blew it out in a huff. "Why, I'm looking for the Answer, of course!"

"The Answer?" cried Tabetha. "To what?"

"Now that is the question!" the funny creature declared, and Tabetha smirked into the steamy night air.

"You're not making any sense at all," she said, watching him flicker from violet to green. Once, when she was six and practicing with her wheelchair in the driveway, she had paused to marvel at the mindless knots of snail-trails glistening in the sun. They went nowhere, had no meaning she could think of, and yet their beauty was unmistakable. Speaking with this Mungling, she thought, was not so different.

The Mungling leaned back and furled his brows. "Not making sense?" he harrumphed before crossing his arms with a frown. "You're an honest girl at least, though you look a bit like an elf. Perhaps it would help if I explained."

"I think it might."

A suspicious light came into the Mungling's eyes and he glanced left and right before whispering, "The empire of Wrush is in terrible danger!"

"Oh!" said Tabetha. "That's horrible!"

The Mungling nodded, scooting closer. "An evil sorcerer named Morlac has hidden our Answer, and we are doomed unless the new empress can find it."

"And you think I have the Answer?"

"It's my job to find out, and as quickly as possible," he said. "If I don't bring the new empress back to Etherios in time, I'm afraid Morlac will take over the empire."

An evil sorcerer? An empress? An Answer without a question? Tabetha's mind spun; it became a wilderness of confusion. She had only just arrived in this strange new world, and already an electric worm wished to rush her off to a floating city on some wild adventure. This was crazy!

Tabetha looked straight into the Mungling's sun-bright eyes. "Are you telling me," she said, "if I go with you to Etherios and find the Answer you're looking for, then I'll become the Empress of Wrush?"

"Absolutely," said the Mungling as he wriggled down from her bed. He was glowing extra bright in his excitement. "Find the Answer. Empress of Wrush. And what's more, you'll save the entire empire from Morlac!" From a bag at his side, the Mungling withdrew a pair of stirrups and a saddle, which he threw over his back so Tabetha could ride him like a horse. "Now hop on," he said. "There's no time to lose."

"But you don't understand," Tabetha insisted. "I'm just a little girl! I have no magic. Or Answers. I'm not an empress, or special in any kind of way." Tabetha's eyes lowered to her legs, then the empty place beside her bed where her wheelchair once rested. Her voice was barely a whisper. "I can't even walk."

The Mungling leaned in close. "Don't be silly! That's not important!"

"But it is," she said, picking at a loose thread in her lap. "And besides, now I even have a pneumonia."

"A *nemer*—" The Mungling scowled, unable to repeat it. "I don't know what you've got, but if it's heavy, I'll carry it. If it barks, you'll have to leave it behind."

"No," she said. "A pneumonia is when your lungs get all plugged inside and it's hard to breath. But real bad. It happens to people like me, who are already sick and spend a lot of time in bed. It's worse when I'm cold, though. So long as I'm not cold, I'll get better—I think. And so long as I take my medicine."

"Well, that's all very interesting," said the Mungling as he climbed up beside her. "But right now there's no time for all that. You'll have to save your pluggy insides for later, because everyone in Wrush needs you in the floating city."

With that, Tabetha felt his soft nose at her back as he began nudging her toward the edge of the bed. But before she could stop him or speak another word, she heard a loud and terrible sound; a thumping and pounding like so many hearts gone wild, and it was coming from deep in the forest.

"What is that?" she hissed in alarm.

The Mungling froze and whispered one word: "Drums."

Boom! Ba-ba! Boom! Ba-ba! Boom! Ba-ba! And over the pounding of drums, Tabetha heard the horrible shrieks of many strange creatures approaching. Fast.

The Mungling gasped. "Oh my bells . . ." Then louder, "Oh my bells! They've found you already! Quickly, Tabetha! To Etherios! It's the only place you'll be safe!"

Tabetha held out her hand to stop him. "Safe from what?"

The Mungling's face tightened with fear.

"The Gwybies!" he cried. "The Gwybies are coming!"

Then the most remarkable thing took place.

A word to the wise.

When escaping from crocodiles, it is important to run in a zigzag motion. Crocodiles are unable to do this. Zigzagging will confuse their dinosaurian brains, and their stumpy legs will find the movement unnatural.

Do not make the mistake of running zigzag from a bear, however, or he will eat you. Instead run crosswise along the steep slope of a mountain, and the bear will lose his balance and tumble.

In a way, running from Gwybies is a simpler affair, as you have nothing in particular to keep in mind. You may do as you like. Run zigzag, run crosswise, flap your arms like a bird. It makes little difference, as the Gwybie is still going to catch you. Unless, of course, you find your way onto the saddled back of a Mungling.

With a gasp and a grunt, Tabetha heaved herself into the saddle and snatched hold of the Mungling's reins. He took off like a slingshot. Tabetha's head whipped back. She had no idea the Mungling could move so swiftly through the jungle. Vines lashed at her face and scraped her arms. Moonlight poked through the forest in long yellow bars, but the shadows remained thick and snarling. Red eyes shone from deep in the woods, and Tabetha leaned forward on her new friend, feeling both excited and frightened at once.

Could this really be happening? Was this a dream? Only this morning Tabetha was writing stories, alone on her birthday in a hospital. Now she was on the adventure of a lifetime!

Just then, the Mungling tipped his head back and called out to her. "Hold on tight!" he shouted. "The danger has only begun. We have a long way to go, and no idea how to get there!"

"You mean you don't know where you're going?" Tabetha called back.

"I know exactly where we're going!" he answered. "I just don't know where that is!"

Crazy little creature! What was he babbling about now? "That makes no sense," she argued. "I thought we were going to a floating city!"

"Yes, yes! But because it's floating, the city is never in the same place twice!"

Tabetha saw gleaming eyes and long, twisting horns dart across their path and disappear into the shadows.

Gwybies . . .

Her stomach knotted with dread. "If Etherios is never in the same place twice, then how will we ever find it?"

"We'll just keep moving," the Mungling shouted. "Sooner or later, the city will find us. It usually works!"

The Mungling sped up, and Tabetha felt the wind claw at her hair. It drew stinging tears from her eyes, and then she smelled them, the Gwybies. An awful stink, like wet dogs in the mud. She caught a glimpse of one's tail as it whipped through the brush, long and hairless like a rat's. The Mungling pulled hard to the right, veering from the path. Leaves as huge as elephant's ears slapped at Tabetha's face as she and the Mungling raced through the jungle, finally breaking free into a clearing.

All around her, Tabetha saw crumbling old walls and half-toppled towers. Jungle roots swallowed it all like a beast. An ancient temple, she realized. Just like in books! Here and there she saw the huge heads of statues stretching up through the vines, or else strapped down to the earth as by tentacles. *How long*, she wondered, *since another person had been here?*

The Mungling dashed through the ruins as though he knew where to go. He leaped over tumbled blocks and slipped between branches. Suddenly Tabetha saw something up ahead. It was a ring of tall stones, and the Mungling raced straight toward them. He halted when he reached the ring's center.

Now, I should pause here a moment. I should explain a little more of these ruins. It will help you to understand what comes next.

You see, there was once a tree there in Wrush, a very old tree. It was known to all in the Great Forest as The Lantern. It was quite stout at the base with thick limbs up above, and its leaves glowed at the height of midsummer. Like all great trees everywhere, The Lantern was much loved, and the forest creatures gathered her glowing leaves for their tea. But those days have long passed. The Lantern is no more.

Nothing is even left to mark it, I am told, but a few stones in a ring, looking very much like those circling Tabetha.

"We'll be safe here," the Mungling panted, while Tabetha touched a tall grey slab at her side. The stones stood tilting and smooth, without any sign of a roof. They were like a ring of pillars and the stars shone bright above. "Have you ever played Tag?" the Mungling asked Tabetha between breaths.

"Yes. But a long time ago."

"This ring of stones is like a magical Home Base. They say something great and powerful once lived in this spot. Something pure. Now no Gwybies will come close enough for harm. Trust me."

All around them, beyond the protective tall stones, the trees of the forest laced the dark sky. Tabetha twisted in place, peering into the surrounding woods. Everywhere she turned, red eyes gleamed back from the gloom. Horns flashed in the moonlight, and Tabetha heard growling. She trembled with fear.

"What are Gwybies, anyway?" she asked. "I've never heard of such things."

There was a loud crash, and the Mungling spun. Somewhere amid the ruins there was howling and shrieking. The Gwybies were fighting among themselves. The Mungling let out a long, slow breath. "The empire of Wrush," he finally said, "was created by children like you, Tabetha. Magical pens were sent out all through your world so that whenever a child wrote with one, a special thing happened."

"What was it that happened?" Tabetha asked, watching the countless shiny eyes that circled her in the shadows. She could almost feel the forest crawling about her.

"The special thing that happened was Wrush," the Mungling said. "Each time a child wrote with a magic pen, our world grew bigger. Whatever the child described became part of our empire."

Tabetha thought back to all the stories she had written that day. Now all of them were here. Alive and real. For the thousandth time, she wished she had an older brother, someone stronger and wise. Someone to protect her.

"But now Morlac, the evil sorcerer I told you about, he's taking over our empire," the Mungling said. "He created an army of monsters to help him."

Tabetha took in a shuddering breath. "You mean the Gwybies, don't you?" Their smell was stronger. They were nearing.

"That's right, Tabetha." The Mungling's voice went flat. "I mean the Gwybies. Morlac created the Gwybies."

In that very moment, the first of them could be seen. Shirking off their fear of the stones, the creatures crept near, breaking free of the forest's dark cover. Tabetha saw their hideous fangs as they pushed up on two legs. She saw the matted hair of their chests. They howled, and the Mungling took a step back.

Then the most remarkable thing took place. It was so unexpected Tabetha distrusted her eyes, only believing when the

Gwybies fell still. The sky lit up, as though from a thousand low stars, and these stars grew into glittering leaves. Then up from the ground, right there in the ring, right there beneath the Mungling's six legs, the golden outline of a tree pushed and twisted around them, then stretched up and up into the night.

It was no more than a ghost, this tree, yet tremendous in size. The Gwybies cringed beneath its glowing height. Then the Mungling startled at a new sound in the forest. There was a crash, and the Gwybies shrunk back in alarm.

"We're saved!" cried the Mungling as the forest began to shake. "He must have seen the glow of this tree!"

"He?" muttered Tabetha. "Who is it that's coming?"

Then she saw two enormous hands, two tractor-tire fists, grasp distant treetops and throw their branches aside.

You would be amazed what a person can see when he's twenty-foot-four.

The giant!" Tabetha whooped with joy. "He's come! He's come!"

"Aaaaaaaarrrrrrgggggg!" the giant thundered as he slapped through the trees. "Get back, you vile little rodents! Back, or I'll thump you for sure!" The giant lifted a mighty war-hammer high into the air and then pounded the ground with a sound like a bomb blast. The earth shook so hard, the tall stones of the magical ring began to sway. The giant roared again and the Gwybies scattered and scampered back into the shadows, their long tails tucked between hairy legs. When not one monster was left, the giant turned to Tabetha and the Mungling, his body towering over the stone ring.

"Worse than a bowl full of stink, those Gwybies." He hooked the hammer to his belt. "I never did like to see them up close."

He stretched out a hand to brush the ghostly leaves of the tree and they faded, slowly, back into the night.

"Oh, thank you! Thank you so much!" Tabetha cried as the giant crouched low. He held out his huge finger and she hugged it tight. "I thought we might be stuck here forever," she said.

The giant smiled. "Not likely," he replied. "That was no ordinary tree. That was The Lantern from days of old. And whatever the Mungling may have told you, this ring is not a safe place for all. That The Lantern came for you, Tabetha, is no small thing."

The Mungling became excited, thinking this very important. He told Tabetha of a legend, a very old legend he had only just now remembered. It was about a girl and a tree and endless worlds in peril, but the legend's ending had been lost long ago. The giant disagreed. "The end wasn't lost," he said. "The story has simply never been finished. It is a tale that still awaits its conclusion."

Talk of this legend sparked something deep inside Tabetha, but she was unsure what to make of it. In the end she was left, for no special reason, with thoughts of the blue hill from her dream earlier that day.

"But your cat," she said with sudden unease. "Did he get left behind?"

"Don't you worry about that," said the giant, and she saw that grin cross his face, that all-knowing grin. "Leave Elsewhere elsewhere; your concern is right here. Wrush is an empire filled to bursting with wonder, but its dangers are too many to ignore. Morlac has grown strong. His Gwybies are everywhere, and this forest is no place for a young girl traveling at night. Are you two actually headed somewhere, or just out for a little wander with monsters?"

"We're going to Etherios," she answered. "To see if I can find the Answer."

"And become the empress!" the Mungling declared. "She may be the one to save us all!"

That made Tabetha feel shy. She still wasn't sure about all this. "But we seem to be having trouble finding anything but trouble right now," she said.

"Not to worry," rumbled the giant as he stood up tall in the moonlight. "I can make out Etherios from here."

"Really?"

"Sure! You would be amazed what a person can see when he's twenty-foot-four."

The Mungling wiggled up closer to the giant's boot. "Seeing as how you're out for a wander yourself, perhaps you'd like to give us a hand? Tabetha here still needs to save the world, and it is getting on toward morning and all . . ."

"Me?" Tabetha choked on the word. "Save the world?"

But the Mungling plowed on. ". . . and with all those Gwybies about, well, it seems like having a giant around might be useful. What do you say?"

"To Etherios, then!" boomed the giant. "I'd take the new empress to the moon if she asked!" Tabetha wanted to tell him she wasn't the new empress yet. Nor was she big enough or strong enough to save anyone from anything. But before she could argue, the giant scooped her and the Mungling into his hands.

"No Gwybies will bother you so long as you're with me," the giant bellowed, and in the blink of an eye, Tabetha was riding high above the jungle on a giant's shoulder. Looking out over the trees, which appeared steamed-broccoli-green in the moonlight, she saw ice-capped mountains rising in the distance. The forest sounds were a thrum of soft music in her ears, and she was happy. Wrush, she realized all at once and with force, was a place beyond all compare.

"Look! Sky Herds!" the giant said as he pointed to the clouds. Tabetha saw hundreds of them, all shaped like fluffy sheep. A Cloud Shepherd strode beside them, tall and strong, with a long, fluffy beard and a staff. Together they marched through the sky.

"Even the Sky Herds won't be safe when Morlac takes over," the Mungling said. Thinking about that made Tabetha sad. So much so that it surprised her. She had only just discovered this world, this wonder, and it was far too special to let some evil sorcerer destroy it.

Well, I could cry over it all night, she thought, a small smile crossing her face, *but the crickets will do that for me . . .*

"I'll help," she announced, her decision swift and final.

"Now that's the spirit!" The Mungling burned bright as a lightbulb.

"I'll do whatever I can," Tabetha said. "But that may not be very much."

"You might be surprised," said the giant. "Here in Wrush, real strength isn't in big muscles or fast legs. It's in the heart." He tapped his massive chest. "That's why I think you should meet my brother."

"Your brother?" she said, and the giant pointed to the snowy peaks beyond.

"That's his home way up there. Deep in the mountains of Wrush."

"But why should I go there if I'm needed in the city?"

"Maybe not now," said the giant. "Maybe not tonight, but one day, I promise." That mysterious grin returned. *You really need to meet my brother.*"

Upon these words, the giant stopped. They were in the crease of a valley, and the trees had grown sparse. Jagged mountains stretched skyward like cliffs. Tabetha could see the leading edge of a city, hovering high in the air, drifting slowly toward them from between two snowy crags.

"Etherios!" the Mungling cried. It hung like a puppet beneath the Cloud Shepherd and his flock. The whole city seemed to float along as if connected to the clouds by invisible strings. Tabetha and the Mungling prepared to head straight to the city when they noticed the river directly crossing their path. A raging river of melted gold.

"Amazing!" Tabetha cried. The river glittered and shone. She was suddenly overcome with thirst. "Can I drink it?"

"No!" the giant boomed, then in a gentler voice added, "It's beautiful, I know. But cursed."

Thirstier than she could ever remember, Tabetha was reminded of shampoo and lip gloss, cans of freshly opened paint, all those inedible delights that took so much strength not to taste.

"What would happen?" she asked. "If someone tried to drink it, I mean. Would they get sick?"

"Dear bells, no! It's much more terrible than that." The Mungling's eyes became huge and bright. "If so much as one drop crosses your lips, you'll speak in riddles for a hundred years!"

Tabetha could admit to having once sampled some tree sap, which had looked just like pure honey, and maybe even barfed a little after nibbling blue soap. But that was all a long time ago. She was much, much older now, and felt quite certain she could resist the river's temptation.

"How will we cross, then?" she asked.

The giant set her and the Mungling down within view of the river's low bank. "You'll have to cross the Bridge of Conundros," he said, pointing to a slender arch of stone that stretched across the rushing, golden waters. "Me, I'm too big to cross that narrow thing. Looks like you and the Mungling will have to go on to Etherios without me."

The bridge certainly was narrow, and it had no railings or bars. The Conundric River flowed swiftly beneath. "Is it even safe?" Tabetha asked.

The giant waggled his hand. "Sort of."

"The real danger," he added, his eyes fixed on the far bank, "is what lies on the other side."

Tabetha looked again to the bridge. This time, she let her eyes span its full length. She gasped when she saw the far side. What she had thought at first to be trees were not trees at all, but a forest of enormous mushrooms! They were bunched and clustered so thick over there, Tabetha could see no path going through. She asked if there might be more Gwybies.

"Gwybies?" repeated the giant. "You'll be lucky to find nothing worse. There are things in that grove—dreadful things—wicked creatures too wicked to name."

Tabetha gulped as though swallowing a bug.

"But the Mungling is as good a companion as any," the giant went on. "He's loyal, I can see, which makes him dear. Now be off. No point in hanging around here. Morlac won't be far behind." He gave that mysterious grin and a wink as he turned. "Don't worry, Tabetha. I believe I'll see you once more before the end."

The end? Tabetha felt something pinch with these words. What could the giant mean by *the end?* She watched him wade back into the trees, his head and shoulders floating over dark tree tops.

Then all at once, like putting on a backpack of bricks, Tabetha felt the full weight of her task. She realized a whole empire was counting on her, a little girl, to become something she wasn't. To find an Answer she didn't know. To save them from the very things she feared.

But why? Why should she be the empress? She looked to the Mungling and searched his face for a clue. What she found was even more unexpected.

The Mungling pulsed again, and from deep in his eyes a clear image came forth. It was the blue hill she often climbed in her dreams. It was brighter than ever—a real thing in her mind. She wondered if the Mungling could see it too.

"I'm ready." Tabetha shifted forward in her saddle. "Let's cross this bridge before I lose my nerve."

The Mungling clucked, flashed from violet to blue, then began his approach to the Bridge of Conundros. Immediately Tabetha had the strange feeling this bridge might be more dangerous than it appeared. The rushing of the river grew louder. They reached its low bank and Tabetha peered down over the edge. The golden waves sloshed and roared yet were more inviting than ever. She wanted to drink from the river right then.

Shampoo and lip gloss. Shampoo and lip gloss . . .

She tried to force back the gnawing urge to drink. She imagined bitter tastes on her tongue; she imagined poisonous hiccups. But the draw of the river only grew stronger. Suddenly Tabetha noticed someone was singing.

"Is that you, Mungling? Your voice is enchanting."

"That's not me," said the Mungling. "It's the magic of the river. Plug your ears or it will pull you in!"

Tabetha tried to do as she was told, but it was simply no use. The riversong still found its way in. She could feel long ghostly fingers reaching up from the banks, gently nudging her toward the delicious water. The singing was so dreamy, the water so fresh. Even the Mungling was now caught in its spell. Tabetha could hear him humming to the song as he drifted closer to the river. Then cool droplets were splashing her arms. Just one moment more and she could drink.

Her throat was so dry, the water so close. She hummed softly aloud, her eyes peacefully closed. The Mungling stirred the shimmering shallows with a finger.

"I have been given the seeds to a mountain and a zebra's bold stripes!"

There was once a time, I am told, when the Conundric River flowed fresh. When the goodfolk of Wrush fished from its shores. Then down from the mountains a new evil appeared and turned the river foul with old magic. This evil was a Thwork, which is the proper name for a dragon when it has declared itself Master of the Bridge.

And it was just such a dragon that Tabetha was about to meet.

"What's that?" she cried, snapping free of the river's spell. The sound of three magic horns warbled and pierced the night air, bending the darkness like water before her.

"A Thwork!" the Mungling gasped, and Tabetha's eyes grew wide. She gripped the saddle hard in pure fright. Rising before her was the heaving bulk of some beast. A three-headed dragon on errand from nightmares.

The Thwork had scales red as fire, and they clicked when he moved. He stretched out across the foot of the bridge. His muscles were steel cords; his eyes were dark rubies. Three heads writhed at the end of long, furry necks, and his wings folded flat against his back.

"Mmmmmmmmmmmmmmh," the dragon thrummed from deep in his throat. Tabetha felt the ground tremble beneath her. Again the dragon raised up the enchanted horns and released their strange call, a sound like voices pressed through the black throat of space.

Barrr- rooooOOOOO!

"We are the Masters of the Bridge of Conundros!" The three heads spoke as one, their voices like hissing steam. "No one may cross this river without our permission!" Slaver dripped from their talon-like teeth, and Tabetha turned her eyes away in fear.

Then she remembered her promise. *I'll help,* she had told her new friends. *I'll help, even if that means facing a . . .*

Tabetha turned back to the Thwork. She urged the Mungling forward. "My name is Tabetha Bright," she explained from atop her saddle. "My friend here is a Mungling who has come to take me to Etherios. The goodfolk of Wrush are there waiting for us, and if we don't arrive soon, a very evil sorcerer named Morlac may destroy your empire. So if you don't mind," she said, "we would be very grateful if you let us pass."

There was silence.

Then all at once the air convulsed with harsh laughter as the Thwork clutched his huge belly and roared. "Those of Etherios are waiting for *you?*" His crimson scales glimmered as he leaned forward in the moonlight. "Why, you're just a tiny girl! What could you possibly do to help our empire?"

"To be honest," she said, "they think I might be the new Empress of Wrush. But only if I can find the Answer."

Upon these words the Thwork stopped laughing. He studied Tabetha long and hard. Tabetha wasn't sure if he meant to swallow her whole or sample her bit by bit.

"The Empress of Wrush, huh?" the meanest-looking of the three heads spat. "Now that would make an interesting meal." The Thwork let out a low growl. "But because you seek the Answer, we shall let you pass. You and your Mungling may cross the Bridge of Conundros."

"Oh! That's very kind of you!" said Tabetha, sharing a smile with the Mungling. "We really don't know how to thank you."

"Oh, but *we* do," all three heads said at once. "You can thank us by paying the toll." The Thwork's mouths twisted into wide, hungry smiles. The long daggers of teeth clacked together like sheers.

"A toll?" said Tabetha. "You mean I have to pay you to cross the bridge?" She patted her pockets to show they were empty. "But I haven't got any money. Nothing at all, really, to offer you. Except maybe this pen." She held it up for the dragon to see.

"A pen!" the Thwork roared, blowing hot steam from his snouts. "What would a Thwork do with a child's filthy toy? Bah! There is no greedier creature in all this empire than a Thwork! Now, you must bring three gifts. One for each of us," he demanded. "Since you have nothing to offer now, you must go and find whatever we ask for."

Tabetha looked to the Mungling, who was shaking his head. "No!" he whispered in warning. "Never trust a Thwork. They're tricky as can be, and smart!"

But Tabetha felt the need to hurry on and could see no other choice. Tricky or not, the Thwork blocked their only passage across the river. Tabetha took a deep breath, sitting up straight in the saddle. "We'll do it," she said in her bravest voice. "Whatever you ask. Name your three gifts and we'll bring them."

The Thwork grinned hungrily. The Mungling scuttled backward. "Oh, yes! And one more thing before you agree," the dragon added as he hunched near. "If you fail, little Tabetha, we will devour you piece by piece!"

$$\mathcal{R}_{\langle}$$

"Now you've done it," said the Mungling to Tabetha. "No one can outsmart a Thwork. How do you hope to get past him?" He shook his chubby head in dismay.

Before Tabetha could answer, the first of the Thwork's three heads bent low, staring Tabetha straight in the eye. "So! You think you're brave, do you? Think you can bring me what I ask?"

Tabetha met his gaze. She nodded.

"Very well, then," the first head replied as he straightened his long neck. He stroked his wispy, white beard in thought. "I happen to have a special gift in mind already. Ever since I was a young Thworkling, I've wanted one thing."

He looked to the sky, where tiny points twinkled yellow and white.

"The stars!" he hissed. "Of course no one has ever managed to bring them to me. Still, this is my request. Bring me the stars in the palm of your hand, little Tabetha. Or I shall start on your ears for supper!"

The Mungling gasped. "But that's impossible!"

"Nonetheless, I want them," said the Thwork.

Tabetha fell quiet. She chewed her lip in thought. "So he wants the stars in the palm of my hand," she muttered to herself. Her legs were so weak she couldn't climb out of her own bed, let alone climb up to the stars. So how would she ever capture one?

Tabetha found herself going deep inside, toward that magic place where her stories were born. A fountain waited there, a shining spout of creativity. To touch it was to let her imagination in. She felt it climb up through her chest and across the long fields of her mind. It poured out through her eyes into the world around her, suddenly latching upon a glowing idea.

"Mungling," she called. "Do you see that puddle beside the bridge?"

The Mungling nodded eagerly.

"Please take me there."

The Mungling did as he was asked, clucking to himself in excitement. When he reached the puddle, Tabetha leaned over her friend's side. She scooped up a handful of water between the palms of her two hands.

"There you are," she said to the Thwork with a smile. "The star you asked for. Several of them, actually."

"What!" the first head roared. "What's this you say?" He bent over the water pooled in Tabetha's hands and sure enough, the stars' reflection twinkled back at him.

"Hold out your claws and I'll give them to you," Tabetha offered. Very carefully, the Thwork did just that, and as Tabetha passed him the stars, she saw the faintest smile ripple across his toothy lips. He said nothing, but stared in wonder.

"Ha!" the second head piped up. "So you are both brave and clever! But it will take more than that, little Tabetha, to bring me the gift I'm about to ask for."

e

"All my life," the Thwork's second head explained, "I've searched and I've searched for one single treasure. Never has it been found. If you can bring this one thing to me now, I will be satisfied. But I warn you. If you fail, little Tabetha, I will snack on your toes for breakfast!"

"I can't promise you anything," said Tabetha. "But I will do my very best."

The Thwork grunted. "Then bring me a song."

Did he say a song? Well that will be easy, Tabetha thought. She knew lots of songs already.

"Bring me a song," the Thwork repeated, "that is sung by neither mouth nor lips."

Oh, thought Tabetha. That sounded quite a bit harder. Still, she had agreed to do her very best, and that's exactly what she meant to do.

"He must mean the river song," said the Mungling, and at those words the Thwork sneered.

"I do not mean the river song!" he snapped. "For the river is already mine! If you wish to cross it to Etherios, then go now and return only when my gift is found."

Tabetha agreed she would, pulling the Mungling back from the bridge. "So this Thwork wants a song that has no singer," she murmured aloud, gripping the reins. But did such a thing even exist?

"This second head looks much hungrier than the first," the Mungling commented. "This riddle is much harder too. How exactly did you solve the last one, Tabetha?"

"By accident," she said. "I just went deep inside myself, and suddenly I had the answer."

"Well, can't you just 'by accident' again?" said the Mungling.

Tabetha wasn't sure. But perhaps she could find that fountain again, deep inside, and then let creativity lead the way. It had worked the first time. Maybe it could work again.

Tabetha relaxed. She felt all her muscles go loose as jelly. Her breathing slowed as she sunk deep within, her creativity spreading broad as a lake. She noticed the chirping of crickets and the cool of night against skin. She noticed the perfume of moist earth, the perfect brushstrokes on a moth, and the way dewdrops shone like diamonds in the moonlight.

Then Tabetha noticed something else.

"Do you see how the fireflies gather high on that ledge?" She pointed so the Mungling could see. "Up there," she said, "where that tall cliff overlooks the river."

The Mungling nodded.

"Take me there," she whispered.

At once they were off, the Mungling climbing the steep path. When they reached the top of the cliff, the Mungling peered over the edge. "I don't know what you plan to do," he said, offering Tabetha a bright grin. "But I'm beginning to think that if anyone could outsmart a Thwork, it just might be you."

Tabetha held up her hands. Fireflies danced circles about them, winking like sparks between her fingers. The mountains around her were tall and dark. The wind blew lightly. Somewhere far away, thunder rolled through silvery clouds. Tabetha began to sing . . .

> *The crumpled old man with a heart of gold*
> *He gives it away and so never grows old*
> *For ninety-nine years his stories are told*
> *And the children enjoy them all day.*

> *The crumpled old man who plants a tree*
> *The fruit that it bears he'll never see*
> *But he doesn't cry, for you and me*
> *Will eat of his gift one day.*

On and on she sang, lifting her voice to the mountains. The fireflies twirled and flashed, and the moment Tabetha stopped, all the forest fell silent with her. Every fox and bat went still as can be. The owls left off from their hooting. And down on the bridge below, even the Thwork stood quiet, watching and waiting for his gift.

Then it came.

Slowly at first, it rolled back down from icy peaks. It was so quiet Tabetha could barely hear it. But soon it grew louder. And louder. And then louder still, until all the valley was alive with her echo:

> The crumpled old man with a heart of gold!
> He gives it away and so never grows old!
> For ninety-nine years his stories are told!
> And the children enjoy them all day!

Again and again the mountains repeated her song. The Thwork's bearded jaw fell open in amazement.

"You did it!" cheered the Mungling. "You found the song that has no singer!"

"I guess I did," said Tabetha, feeling quite surprised at herself. She peered over the cliff's edge. "But we better hurry back down to the Thwork," she said. "Don't forget, time is running out and we still have one more gift to bring him before we can cross the Bridge of Conundros." She glanced down at the bridge, her stomach roiling with dread. "And that last Thwork looks the meanest of all."

$\mathcal{C}$

Tabetha and the Mungling halted at the foot of the bridge. She glanced up at the dragon, who was now a towering shadow with the moon like a great yellow disk behind. Tabetha opened her mouth to speak, when suddenly the Thwork reared back on his hind legs and threw wide his red wings. He pumped them until dust swirled like a cyclone. Tabetha gasped. She squinted against the wind. She had never seen such an angry creature!

The Thwork huffed and he roared and he blew his great horn until at last the third—and the meanest—of the three heads leaned in close to Tabetha. Her hair lifted in puffs as he snorted in her ear.

"So, little Tabetha!" the dragon hissed. "It seems you are not just brave and clever, but talented, too! Yet it will take something more to please me. Much more, in fact. You see, I am the greediest Thwork in all this empire, and I already have at least one of everything."

"Everything?" asked Tabetha. "Then you must be a very sad, sad creature to still need something more."

"Enough!" the Thwork bellowed, and Tabetha's cheeks stung from his breath. "I have been given the seeds to a mountain and a zebra's bold stripes! I've been given lightning in a shimmering white egg. I possess the black tears of a Mud Fairy and an emperor's jeweled sword. But if you wish to cross this bridge, little Tabetha, then you must find and bring to me one thing. The one thing in all of this empire I have never been given."

Tabetha looked up at the Thwork. Behind the anger in his eyes she saw his sadness. *How terrible it must be,* she thought, *to have everything and still not be satisfied.* Without saying a word, Tabetha waved the Thwork closer.

"What is it?" he sneered as he bent down low. "Do you think you can give me what no one else can?"

"Come closer," was all Tabetha said, and suddenly the Thwork looked nervous. His eyes went big and darted side to side.

"Closer still," whispered Tabetha, and when the dragon's beard was so near that it swished at her cheek, Tabetha stretched up high in her saddle.

And gave
      the dragon
            a kiss.

It would be very easy, she realized, to get lost in a place such as this.

I can't believe it," the Mungling chirped as he and Tabetha crossed the Bridge of Conundros. Tabetha looked back over her shoulder and saw the Thwork waving good-bye from the riverbank. "I just can't believe it," the Mungling repeated. "Not only did you outsmart a three-headed Thwork and earn his friendship, but he gave *you* a gift! Incredible! No one will ever believe this." He cranked his head around, a curious look on his face. "So. What did he give you?"

Tabetha held up a little red bottle. "The Thwork called it Onion Perfume."

"Yuck!" said the Mungling. "That sounds terrible!"

Tabetha pressed down on the cap and let out a tiny spray. Instantly her eyes began to water. "Whew!" She wiped the tears from her cheeks with a sleeve. She frowned at the bottle in her hand. "It certainly wasn't at the top of my birthday list. But a gift is a gift, I suppose, and he said it might be helpful later. How much further to Etherios, anyway?"

At that moment, the Mungling halted. They had reached the far bank of the river. Together, Tabetha and the Mungling craned their necks to stare up into the overgrown thickets of mushrooms.

"This way, I'm sure," said the Mungling as he squeezed nervously onto a narrow trail. "Etherios should be just through here. Supposing it hasn't floated away again, that is."

Tremendous mushrooms pressed down on Tabetha from all around. They smelled of wetness and rot. The ground was carpeted in thick green moss, and Tabetha heard water dripping from the mushrooms' enormous caps. It would be very easy, she realized, to get lost in a place such as this.

"These stalks are as big around as tree trunks." The Mungling's voice echoed as he slipped between a particularly large mushroom and a moss-covered boulder. But Tabetha was watching a blue fog settle over the grove. It clung to her skin, heavy and thick, and made her shudder with an icky feeling inside. "It's like when my mom wipes my face with licked napkins," she complained, and then the Mungling shuddered too and glowed brighter with fear, adding an eerie glow to the fog all around them.

Small creatures whooped from atop the caps of huge toadstools, leaping from one to the next as though over rooftops.

Others huddled in wet shadows, diving deep into mosses as Tabetha and the Mungling approached. The dampness of this place made Tabetha's chest ache. She worried about her pneumonia.

"Yes, yes, they call this place Grimpkins' Hollow." The Mungling snorted anxiously. "Yes, Grimpkins' Hollow. Not a place to linger, that's for sure."

Then something big flashed through the mists. Tabetha hugged herself tight. "I don't think I like this place, Mungling. Not one bit. Could we please hurry through?"

The Mungling opened his mouth to answer, when a burst of lunatic, high-pitched laughter spiked through the mist.

Aah! Hah hah hah hah!

The Mungling froze. "Whatever you do, Tabetha, do not laugh back," he warned. "A Grimpkin will do anything he can to make you laugh, and once you start, you'll never stop. You'll be stuck here in these woods forever, cackling with the rest of them."

"A Grimpkin?" whispered Tabetha, her fretful eyes searching the woods. "What's a Grimpkin?"

"Joy Gobblers," the Mungling replied. "Grimpkins eat laughter instead of food. They'll feed you enchanted tea by the jugfull till you're all tickly inside, then they'll gobble up your joy until there's not one chuckle left. You'll be all dried up like a raisin."

"Hey, Tabetha! Look at me!" blurted a new voice. Then the funniest little man swung down from a toadstool's cap. His hair was white and wild and seemed to sprout from his head in every which way. His eyes were big and googly, and he wore the silliest grin from ear to ear. He hung upside down from the mushroom's edge, swinging back and forth, and then he fell flat on his face.

Tabetha covered her mouth to keep from giggling. "Turn away!" whispered the Mungling. "They're far too silly! No one can watch a Grimpkin without laughing!"

Suddenly three more of the little men appeared. They began dancing in circles about Tabetha. "Just give us one little giggle! Just one little taste! We know you've got plenty to spare!"

"Oh my bells!" cried the Mungling as he scurried down the trail. "We've got to get you out of this forest!" But the Grimpkins kept coming, more and more of them. They tumbled over each other in a ridiculous heap, shoving pies made of mud in their faces.

"Come with us!" they taunted, and then cackled some more. "We'll tell you jokes till your tears taste like honey!" Tabetha saw Grimpkins belching an opera. They played catch with rotten fruit. They choked on tea and coughed it back through the nose.

Tabetha couldn't take it much longer. The Grimpkins were just too silly! It took every bit of her strength to hold back the laughter. Then all at once, she remembered . . .

The Onion Perfume!

"I'm sorry, Mungling. You're not going to like this," she said as she pulled the little red bottle from her pajama pocket. "Hold your breath if you can, because I promise, this is not going to be the least bit pleasant."

The Grimpkins danced about, cackling and falling over each other like a pile of puppies. Tabetha lifted the bottle of Onion Perfume. She straightened her arm, holding the bottle as far away from herself as she could. "This better be good," she whispered as she sucked in a deep breath. She cranked her head to the side. She squinched up her face up and then . . .

Click. Click.

She squeezed the bottle twice, and a thick grey haze of the foulest perfume squirted into the air. Tabetha gagged as it reached her nose, and her eyes burned like liquid fire. But before long, the onion cloud drifted away from her and the Mungling. It spread out through the forest, washing over the Grimpkins.

Suddenly they didn't seem so silly anymore.

Tabetha sprayed and sprayed until not one drop remained. Instead of cackling, she soon heard a new kind of sound in the forest.

"Look!" shouted the Mungling. "They're crying!"

All around Tabetha, under the mushrooms and atop them, little Grimpkins wiped at their eyes and bawled.

"Just one little morsel!" they sniveled through runny noses. "Just one juicy little giggle before you go!"

But Tabetha and the Mungling slipped down the path, leaving every little Grimpkin behind.

R⅃

"Well, Tabetha, you've done it again," said the Mungling as the forest thinned and the mushrooms grew smaller and smaller.

"For a little girl, you have some big surprises. I wonder what else you might have in store for us."

Tabetha couldn't help but smile. "No little girl could ask for a braver friend," she said as she rubbed the top of his gleaming head. "I think we make a pretty good team."

The Mungling chatted on as they wove through the forest. He talked about the arrogance of unicorns and the best way to peel a ripe hair-fruit. They sucked on damp moss to cool their parched throats, and Tabetha found herself wondering what her parents, a world away, would think of their eight-year-old daughter running wild with Munglings and Grimpkins and sorcerers. The thought of her mother's surprise made her snicker aloud.

"What's so funny?" asked the Mungling.

Tabetha answered with a squeeze.

Soon the fog and the mushrooms of Grimpkins' Hollow gave way to oak trees and maples. The night was nearly over. The sun would be rising soon. Suddenly Tabetha was struck with a thought: *My medicine! How could I forget?* She needed her medicine every day at noon or else she would never get better, and certainly the time for her last dose had passed.

She pressed down on the watch's light, peering into the screen. But to her surprise, only a few minutes had elapsed since she had left the hospital. How strange! *Time must move differently here in Wrush,* she realized, which meant she could still return to Earth in time for her medicine. Relieved, she set her alarm to remind her when to leave.

So Tabetha and the Mungling traveled on for a time, taking in the soft scent of the dark woods, until something else occurred to her. "Mungling," she said abruptly. "I just realized something."

"Yes, yes? And what is that?"

"I don't even know your name," she said.

The Mungling paused. She heard him sniffle. "Neither do I," he said. "At least, if I ever had a name, I've forgotten it."

"Maybe if you just stand on your head and hold your breath you'll remember," Tabetha suggested. "It works for me when I've forgotten something."

"No, no. I've already tried." The Mungling appeared very upset. "You see, I'm not actually from the empire of Wrush."

"You're not? Then where do you come from?"

"Your world," said the Mungling.

"Really?" Tabetha gave him a look of surprise. "But I've never seen your kind before."

"That's because we Munglings live in nests, high up in the sun," he explained. "Sun-wyrms, you could call us. If you lay on your back on a clear blue day, you might see us squirting about. Like tiny lights flitting through sky."

"Then I have seen you!"

"Oh, yes, I'm sure you have. But since coming to Wrush, I've forgotten my name. Without it, I can never go back home to my own kind."

That made Tabetha sad. She knew what it was to be lonely. So many times she had lain in her hospital bed, waiting for her parents' next visit.

"Do you have any brothers?" she asked him at last. "Any older brothers?"

The Mungling's chin quivered as he scrubbed at his eyes. "Thousands."

"Well, if I ever find the Answer and become the Empress of Wrush, then I promise you," Tabetha said as she patted his side, "I'll help you get back to your family. We'll find your name together."

Tabetha saw the first rays of a purple sun burst over the mountains, and she felt its warmth on her skin. The trees of the forest slowly faded to meadow. Soon there was only tall grass and streams and fields of red flowers dotting the land. "How beautiful!" she exclaimed. Then she looked up.

"Oh my gosh!" she cried.

"Etherios!" announced the Mungling as he galloped through the fields. "We've finally made it, Tabetha. We've finally reached the city!"

"I feel more alive today than ever before."

One more thing about Wrush. Something you should probably know: It is considered impolite to point at anything in the sky. I admit, it's a silly tradition, dating back to a time when Wrushic clouds were still dangerous. They were once a bit touchy, you see, about having so little to wear. They struck out at the slightest provocation. But all that has changed now, thanks to the Cloud Shepherd and his flock, and so little Tabetha was not to be blackened by angry lightning as she might have been in the past.

"Look!" she cried out, pointing just overhead, where an entire city floated above the meadow. She saw palaces and gardens and castles and towers. Instead of roads there were swinging ramps that tied each balcony to the next. "I think I'll like this place," Tabetha said through a grin.

The Mungling picked up his pace. "And that," he assured her, "is because all children love magic." One glance skyward and Tabetha knew this was true.

"You know," the sun-wyrm went on, "nothing reminds me of home so much as the first sight of Etherios. All those happy families up there, drinking up the sun. Mother Munglings say there's nothing finer, and they are quite well known for their advice. My own mother, she was wise as could be, and she was very fond of saying, 'If any single day doesn't find me a better person at its end, then I failed to truly live that one.' I think she'd be proud of me today. Proud of us both, actually. What would yours say if she could see you now?"

"I don't know, really," said Tabetha, thoughtful, her eyes still fixed upon the underside of the enormous city above. "But I can say this: I feel more alive today than ever before."

And Tabetha said this because it was true. Because she was happy, sincerely happy, riding atop a Mungling beneath Saturday-colored skies in a world where children know all there is to know. She watched the city float along, her gaze brushing its belly like fingertips against some great white animal in the sky. As the Mungling drew nearer, Tabetha noticed long threads, or strings, with tiny hooks at the end, all dangling from lines beneath the city. They looked like miniature anchors that never quite reached the ground.

She pointed to one. "Mungling," she said. "Are those . . . what are those things?"

"You mean the fishing lines?"

"I guess. Is that what they are? But what good is it fishing in midair?"

"What good?" the Mungling clucked, seeming unsure how to answer. "Well, how else would you catch a fish from a cloud?"

ℛ

A word to the wise.

When defending yourself against an attack from a hungry shark, do not lose your cool. Sharks will sense fear and interpret your thrashing as the movement of prey. It *is* important, however, to fight back. I will teach you.

But first: It is commonly said that a shark's nose is particularly sensitive and a stout blow here will turn his attack. This is a lie. Only those who secretly wish you to be eaten by sharks will say such a thing, and friends of this sort are not to be trusted.

Instead of striking the nose of the shark, make repeated jabs with your fist at the gills, which you can find by carefully measuring one and a half hand widths back from the eye. This will communicate to the shark that you are not helpless and furthermore do not wish to be eaten. He will leave you.

Now, should you one day find yourself in Wrush, remember to forget everything I have just said, as sharks here are land animals and therefore have no gills. Which, coincidentally, explains the very peculiar defense mechanism of another fish, likewise found in Wrush. One that Tabetha was about to discover.

ℛ

The Mungling halted in the meadow. Tabetha gripped his reins in reflex. What looked like a flock of birds hovered out over the tall grass. But they were not birds; they were fish, in fact. A school of flying fish, dashing this way and that. Their skin glittered silver in the morning light.

"Fish!" Tabetha broke into a smile. "Look at them!"

So that's what the hooked lines were for!

"And those aren't just any old trout," the Mungling explained. "Those there are genuine Northern Marsupial Blink Fish, probably the first of the season. They're called Blink Fish because when they get frightened they—"

Tabetha blinked in surprise. "They're gone!" she said as the entire school vanished into thin air. "Your voice must have scared them off."

The Mungling gave her an embarrassed grin.

"Bells and pumpkins!" cried a man's voice from above. "You just blinked my breakfast away!" Tabetha looked up to see who had spoken. To her amazement, she saw a swing hanging beneath the city as though strung from a tree's limb, and in it was a man. A fisherman, in fact. He reeled in his fishing line, muttering angrily to himself. "I've caught barely enough Blinkers for a mouthful. What'll my children say? Oh, dear me. Dear, dear me."

"Ahoy there!" called the Mungling, looking up at the man. "So sorry about the fish! But do you think you could throw down a ladder?"

The man in the swing peered down at them. His face brightened with surprise. "Why, it's the Mungling!" he whooped, slapping a hat against his thigh. "You've finally returned. And it looks like you've brought the new empress!"

Tabetha flinched upon hearing those words. What if she wasn't the empress? What if she couldn't find the Answer? After everything the Mungling had done for her, she would hate to disappoint him now. Even worse, she would be letting the whole empire down and Morlac would be free to conquer Wrush.

A little nervous, she said, "Well, they're sure happy to see you here. I guess wyrms like you must make lots of friends."

"As you can see," he said, still watching the fisherman above, "I'm not truly a wyrm. Wyrms don't have legs. I have six."

"Not a wyrm? I thought that's what you told me."

"I am a Mungling," said the Mungling, "which is just a silly little word meaning *those who don't yet know what they are.*"

"Hmph," said Tabetha, wondering if that made her a Mungling too. For like the Mungling, whom she decided was nothing more than a caterpillar, Tabetha sensed she was slowly changing. Suddenly that huge moth came to mind, that one she'd picked up when she'd first arrived in Wrush, only she felt it now, asleep in her chest—a warm cocoon nearly ready to open.

"I think I'm like you," she said to the Mungling. "I don't really know what I am. Or what I'm supposed to be. But I think all that's about to change." She was quiet for a moment, then thought aloud, "I wonder what it is we're becoming?"

"I think," said the Mungling, "none of us knows all that we are, until the very day we become it."

Tabetha heard something smack the ground beside her. She turned to find a rope ladder dangling from the city above. The fisherman waved from his swing, and the Mungling took hold of the ladder. "Now, don't let go of me!" he shouted as he began to climb. Tabetha wrapped her arms around his squishy neck.

So soon as they reached the top, and before Tabetha could so much as yelp, she felt strong hands grab hold and hoist her from the ladder. Someone—many people, in fact—bounced her high in the air, and she heard much cheering.

"The Mungling's returned!" people shouted with glee, and Tabetha was surprised to find a whole parade of people awaiting them on the steps of a most unusual palace: the Citadel, legendary home of the throne.

"He's come back!" people yelled as they pushed into the palace courtyard. Tabetha saw vines trailing down from high white walls. Every building in the city was white. "And he's brought the young girl!" they cried over and over again, passing her from shoulder to shoulder like a trophy.

The townsfolk rushed forward to greet them. Women twisted flowers into Tabetha's dark hair. Young ones elbowed closer for a view. The elders, excitement bright in their eyes, whispered among themselves of a new empress.

Without warning, the crowd hushed and parted, allowing a huge soldier to approach. He wore a knight's helmet and a long sword at his hip, and this he pushed aside as he crouched to one knee before Tabetha. "My Lady," he breathed, a look of awe upon his bearded face. "Is it true? Is it . . . is it finally true?"

"Is what true?" she asked.

The soldier swallowed, his voice soft with wonder. "Are you the one?"

The crowd grew restless in the space of Tabetha's silence, and then a thousand voices answered for her. "She's the one! She's here at last! The child who would save our empire!"

"Now, now, people!" the Mungling shooed them all away, and allowed Tabetha to be returned to his back. "Young Tabetha has had a very long journey. All night long she's traveled, and she's very tired. I must get her to the Citadel at once." The Mungling pushed his way through the crowd and carried Tabetha up the powder-white steps. Tabetha turned over her shoulder. The last thing she saw was the huge soldier's helmet flashing through sunlight as he sprinted back through the crowd, headed straight for a cluster of bright towers. She lurched forward in her saddle as the Mungling came to a sudden halt.

"At last, little Tabetha," he said at the foot of the Citadel's gate. "We've come to the end of our journey. Inside this palace you will either find the Answer, or you won't. The fate of our empire lies just beyond these doors."

Tabetha swallowed hard. She heard the Mungling's slow exhale.

"Are you ready, then?"

Tabetha gazed up at the Citadel, one hand behind her neck, her mouth hanging open in astonishment. Snowy towers rocketed up into the clouds and serpentine banners snapped in the breeze. Tabetha had been told what to expect, yet nothing could have prepared her for this. From breathtaking turrets down to the mighty twin doors, every inch of this palace had been fashioned from pure *curdite*, or fossilized cloud.

Of course, Tabetha could not have known, but there was a reason for this. You see, reader, the first palace had been made entirely of glass. But the goodfolk of Wrush sung with voices so sweet that the palace shattered upon the very first note. Even to this day the goodfolk use cut crystal for windows, and should you one day visit their land, you'll notice their windows are cloudy and throw rainbows of light.

"A thousand times I've been here," said the Mungling, wagging his head in awe before the palace. "Yet somehow it grows more dazzling with every visit. A true wonder, I'd say. A true wonder, but amazingly, only a pebble in the sand compared to what lies within. So I'll ask you once more." He turned to her. "Are you ready, Tabetha? Are you truly prepared?"

Without answering, she urged him to the enormous twin doors, pausing within their long shadow. Instead of doorknobs, there hung only a stout golden ring. Tabetha stared in silence. Slowly, she reached out. She rested one finger on the cool metal of the ring, marveling at what might lay just beyond.

In just a few moments, she would discover if she really was the Empress of Wrush. She would find out if the giant was right, if a little girl's heart really was big enough to save a whole empire.

Tabetha took the great ring in both hands. A tingle of excitement climbed up from her belly. *Ready,* she mouthed silently, then clacked the ring three times against the hard white doors.

The air glistened faintly. The palace began to hum. The doors swung wide on silent hinges, and a wonderful sweetness washed over her.

The Mungling took one step inside and then paused; Tabetha's heartbeat roared in her ears. Spreading out before them was an enormous hall fit for the finest of kings. Thousands of candles sparkled off curdite walls so that the entire hall dazzled and blazed like a bonfire in a House of Mirrors. Tabetha looked up to the ceiling but felt dizzy with the height. She closed her eyes and drew slow breaths. The palace's inner hall smelled crisp and bright as the air after a summer rain. When she opened her eyes again, she gazed slowly about her. Something, she realized, was not quite right.

"Mungling," she said. "The Citadel is completely empty. Where are all the people? Why do they stay outside?"

"Oh, yes, yes. I'm afraid those times are long gone," he said. "Without an empress to sit upon the throne, no one comes here anymore. And no one will come again until the Answer is found."

Then something caught Tabetha's eye. At the far end of the hall, in the very center of the white tiled floor, she saw a tremendous ball. But this ball was not like any other. It was tall as a man, smooth as water, and completely mirrored so that it reflected everything around it. "What in the world is that?" Tabetha asked as she pointed to the strange globe.

"I don't actually know," said the Mungling. "Nobody does, in fact. It's been there, right where you see it, since the day our empire lost its Answer. We call it simply the Ovidium. But look beyond it. Yes, yes, just over there. What do you see?"

"Whoooaa," Tabetha murmured to herself. "Are those . . . ?" She swallowed, but her mouth had gone dry. "Are those what I think they are?"

High on a platform, just beyond the strange mirrored ball, there sat seven crystal thrones in a row. Six of them, Tabetha saw, seated statues of men and women. "They look so real. Just like people," Tabetha said, then added, "except . . . made of stone."

The Mungling began wiggling his way across the hall as he explained. "They are people," he said as they approached the thrones and their statues. "At least, they were people. Once."

"What happened to them?"

"Like you," said the Mungling, "each of them tried to find the Answer. Each desired to be the ruler of Wrush and so sat in the ruler's throne. But only the true Empress of Wrush can sit upon it and wear the crown. All others will be turned to stone."

Tabetha shuddered at the thought. She knew she was meant to try the same thing.

"Their hearts were not pure and free," the Mungling went on. "Some part of them was greedy. The people you see there secretly wanted a bit of Wrush all for themselves."

"And you think I'm different," said Tabetha.

"The true Empress of Wrush," replied the Mungling, "will be one who has great power but keeps none for herself. She will wear the Orchid Crown, and all things good will serve her. Only then will Wrush find its missing Answer."

Tabetha gulped. The thought of being turned into stone made her chest tighten. Her palms went slick with sweat. She checked her watch without really seeing the time, and then once again, she remembered her promise.

I'll help, she had said, and she meant it still. Even if she couldn't walk. Even if she was ill, and frightened, and only eight years old. Even if she knew nothing about sorcerers, she could still do her best.

Here in Wrush, real strength isn't in big muscles or fast legs, the giant had told her. *Real strength is in the heart . . .*

"Take me to the throne," she told the Mungling.

The Mungling scurried past the Ovidium and up onto the platform where the seven thrones sat. Only one was empty. The others were filled with stony men and women, staring with hard, lifeless eyes. Tabetha found herself studying the last statue. It was a beautiful woman with long, wavy hair. *She looks more like a true empress than I ever will*, Tabetha thought to herself, and yet even the woman's dress had turned to stone.

Tabetha felt unable to pull her eyes from this sight, until she noticed something resting upon the stone woman's head. It was a wreath of white flowers, fresh and bright as if picked that very morning.

"The Orchid Crown," the Mungling said, pointing to the wreath. "Wear it as you sit upon the throne. Only then will we know who Tabetha Bright really is."

Carefully, Tabetha lifted the crown from the statue's head. She set the twisting petals in her lap as the Mungling nudged her into the Crystal Throne. When he finished, he backed away.

Tabetha sat alone with the statues. The wreath tingled in her hands. She was studying its white flowers, considering her task, when a new voice arose. A voice unlike any she'd heard before.

The voice was only a whisper, yet Tabetha heard it all the same. She felt it move inside her, soft and warm, like velvet ribbons passing through her heart. Somehow, without any doubt, Tabetha knew the voice she heard was that of the Crystal Throne.

"So you wish to be the Empress of Wrush, do you?" the throne whispered in her mind.

"Actually, no," Tabetha silently answered. "I only want to help, and *empress* sounds like too big a job for a little girl like me."

"Just a little girl, you say?" The throne seemed to consider her words. "But wasn't it you, just a little girl, who summoned the magic of The Lantern?"

After a shy moment, Tabetha admitted this was so.

"And wasn't it you, just a little girl, who promised to help the Mungling find his name?"

"I suppose I did," said Tabetha, her skin beginning to tingle.

"And wasn't it just a little girl who outsmarted a three-headed Thwork? A little girl who found stars in a mud puddle, who gave voice to the mountains and taught a dragon the real meaning of gifts?"

"It was," Tabetha confessed, her voice breaking on the words.

"And who escaped from the Grimpkins to travel dangerous lands? To seek out an Answer no one else could find?"

Tabetha's heart ached. It felt too full to speak.

The throne's whisper paused. "And who is it that sits here now, in the empress's crystal throne, willing to be turned to stone for only one chance to save an empire?"

Tabetha closed her eyes. "Just a little girl," she said.

A soft breeze reached her from somewhere. Everywhere. Deep down inside, Tabetha knew the throne was smiling.

"Rise, little Tabetha, true Empress of Wrush. Lift the Orchid Crown to your noble head."

Tabetha's eyes began to sting. She placed the flower wreath as she was told. Instantly, a white roar filled the hall as every candle blazed to life, each now a lion with a mane of fire. The lions' praise echoed from the Citadel's every high corner until it seemed the walls themselves sung aloud. And when at last the lions fell quiet and every burning mane was but a candle again, Tabetha Bright brushed at her cheeks with the back of her wrist.

She smiled at the Mungling. She lifted a hand to wave him forward, when to her surprise, a second miracle stole her breath away. Tabetha gripped the arms of her throne, leaning forward in disbelief. The Ovidium was moving! The mirrored ball was rolling right toward her!

The giant globe creaked across the tiles before coming to a halt before the foot of her throne. Its surface shone with countless points of light, each reflecting the candles of the hall. Tabetha saw herself in its mirror, stretched tall and grand. Then all of a sudden, POP!

Tabetha's ears rang as the globe shattered into tiny bits. Countless ravens exploded from it in all directions, filling the Citadel like a fluttering storm. The sound of them was deafening. Then, unexpectedly, they plunged to the floor like falling rain, splashing into liquid colors as they hit.

Tabetha's eyes went wide. She heard the Mungling gasp.

In the very center of the hall stood a boy.

The boy clasped both hands before him with his head bent low. His skin was dark. His head was shaved clean and he wore no shirt, but only a billowy pair of leather trousers. Curvy letters were tattooed across his chest and down the lengths of each arm, forming an unbroken line of strange writing. The boy slowly lifted his head and approached the throne on bare feet.

"Who are you?" Tabetha asked in wonder. The air about his head crackled with power.

"I am the High Wizard of Wrush," the boy said, bowing his head again. "And the only name I've ever had ... is *Answer*."

"How much can one person, even an empress, do all alone?"

Tabetha shook her head in astonishment. She had found the Answer! She had actually found it! Who would have ever guessed Answer was a boy? Joy galloped through her heart like a team of horses. Fireworks lit the corners of her mind. She wanted to shout, *I've found the Answer, and his eyes burn like black suns!* But then he was standing before her, and she sucked in a quick breath. For Tabetha suddenly understood what it was to be face to face with not a boy, but the most powerful wizard in the empire.

"Your Majesty," said the boy-wizard as he bowed from the waist. His voice was much older than he looked. "If you only knew how long I've awaited this moment, to be free of the Ovidium's curse."

Answer rose and closed his eyes.

As if she were under a spell, Tabetha's mind suddenly filled with images of living cramped inside that magic globe. She felt the stifling darkness, the press of hard walls. The thought alone made her want to shriek out loud and gulp fresh air.

Her voice came breathless when she spoke. "But how did Morlac ever trap you in the Ovidium?"

The boy-wizard surprised her with a friendly chuckle. "Now that is a tale!" he said. "But for another time, I think. What matters now is that I was locked away, and only one person in this entire empire had a heart pure enough to free me from my enchanted prison. That person was you, Your Majesty. You've returned the empire's greatest wizard to their people, and on their behalf, I give you thanks."

Upon these words, the boy bowed low again, and Tabetha felt her shyness returning.

"But most of all," Answer said as he straightened, "you've given us the one thing our empire has always lacked. You have given us a good and selfless leader, a true Empress of Wrush. You've granted us the gift of real hope, and for this, I, the highest wizard in all the empire, give you *my* thanks."

This time the boy did not bow low, but instead went down on a knee in deepest gratitude.

"Ask anything of me, and I will serve," he said from the floor.

But Tabetha didn't want anything from him. She just wanted to help.

"I suppose there is one thing you could do," she said after a pause.

"Anything, Your Majesty. Name it."

"All right, then. I would like you to call me Tabetha," she said. "And please, get up from the floor. A lot has changed since I last left my hospital bed. But the best things are still the same. I may now be the Empress of Wrush, but I'm still me. Tabetha Bright."

The boy smiled. Suddenly Tabetha was struck with the strangest thought: that this boy, this wizard, this Answer, was in fact the kind and protective sibling she'd always wished for. She had found the brother of her dreams and her real self in the very same day.

"You prove your worth with every word," Answer replied. His ink-dark eyes twinkled, and she understood he was proud of her. "But as your advisor and guide, I must remind you," he continued, "you are the new empress. Your people are counting on you to stop Morlac and his army of Gwybies."

Tabetha sighed. "I know you're right, but I still don't see how that's possible. How much can one person, even an empress, do all alone?"

"But you're not alone," said the boy-wizard. He laced his fingers together as though hugging a tree. The curvy, tattooed letters began to move. Slowly at first, they swam across his chest, down one arm and up the other. The letters traveled in a ring about his body like a toy train around its track. Tabetha tried to read them but could not, for they lit with golden light and a strange whispering packed the air. "The Empress of Wrush will always have the High Wizard at her side," the boy said with a mischievous grin.

"Oh, yes, yes! And a Mungling too!" chirped the sun-wyrm as he flashed brightly in his excitement.

"I'm grateful," said Tabetha. "Really, I am. But even two friends, as loyal as you are, may not be enough to stop an army."

"That's why you'll have us!" came a strong voice as the doors to the Citadel were thrown wide. The huge soldier she had seen in the courtyard now stood in the entrance. Behind him knelt a thousand soldiers. "My name is Isaac, and I've brought you your force. For what is an empress without an army of her own?"

"An army? Of my own?" Tabetha didn't know what to say. She looked upon the many faces staring up at her in her throne. Then she glanced at her watch—the only hint, I might add, she would ever give of her fatigue. For though she did her best to hide it, I must interrupt here and inform you that Tabetha was not at all well.

Her strength was fast fading, and all along she had been coughing in secret, but complaining was simply not part of her nature. So I tell you now, dear reader, and only because Tabetha would not: It took all of her will, every single bit, to simply remain upright in her throne.

Tabetha drew a deep breath, hearing the wheeze in her lungs. "Well, as your empress, I'm probably supposed to tell you all what to do now." She waved the Mungling closer and climbed atop his back. As if on cue, the alarm on her watch went off, and everyone present gave a look of confusion.

"But it might be better if you all just continue to think for yourselves," she said. "I'll try to come back as soon as I can."

"You're leaving us so soon?" asked Isaac. "You've only just arrived!"

Tabetha went to the Citadel's entrance. She looked up and saw a blue sun rolling high in the sky.

"I belong here, it's true," she said. "But I belong in another place, too. I can't ignore all that I am."

"But stay with us now!" cried Isaac. "Return to your own world when Morlac is defeated!"

"I can't," Tabetha said, and her throat felt thick when she swallowed. With a shuddering breath, she forced back the tears. "Without my medicine, I'll never get better. Besides," she managed one last smile. "I have a strange feeling there's a lot I can do to help you, even from my own world. What that might be, I don't yet know. But one thing is certain. Wherever I go, I'll never be 'just a little girl' again."

$\mathcal{L}$

Tabetha checked her watch again. She had only a few minutes left. The nurses would be bringing her medicine, and if she weren't there . . .

"I'll need paper," Tabetha told the Mungling as they rushed through a small door in the back of the hall, then up a winding spiral of stairs. "And lots of it."

The sun-wyrm hurried her to a private chamber, high in a tower of the Citadel. There, he set her at a wooden table with a stack of paper so tall she could barely reach the top to grab a piece.

As soon as she had taken out her magic pen, she began to write. Dappled mists danced about the pen's tip as she wrote about the hospital where she stayed. She described herself in her room and her family coming to visit. She described Nurse Myrtle scuttling about with her flashlight. She described a small, dreary bed beside a small, dusty window where sunlight poured through like rare gold.

The next thing Tabetha knew, she was curled up in her sheets. She heard voices as visitors passed in the hallway outside her hospital room door. She sat up. "I hope I'm in time," she murmured to herself.

She peered up at the big clock *tick-ticking* above the door. One minute to noon. She had barely made it. She breathed a sigh of relief as she slumped back against her pillow. Then memories of Wrush brought a smile to her face. "What a birthday!" she cried aloud as she slapped the sheets beside her.

Tabetha pushed herself up on one elbow, gazing excitedly about the room, but the trees and flowers from this morning were all gone. The gorilla was gone too, and there was, of course, no sign of the giant. With a flash of disappointment, it occurred to Tabetha that she had no proof whatsoever that she'd ever left this bed. Should someone have asked—her mother, for example—Tabetha would have nothing but a few scratches to show for all her wild adventures. A part of her wished she had some kind of souvenir. Something she could look at. To remember.

But as Tabetha got thinking, she realized this: Nothing in her life had been fixed by the journey. She still couldn't walk. She still lived alone in a hospital while her parents lived in their home. She still had pneumonia, which kept her weak and in bed. For all the magic she'd encountered in her travels, it still wasn't enough to spill over into her own world.

Yet deep down inside, Tabetha Bright knew that something, a part of her she could neither see nor touch, was changed. Maybe even forever. The thrill of this discovery sent delicious shivers up her spine. She startled, turning toward a sound across the room.

Tabetha, blinking twice in surprise, realized she was not alone. Pushed up against the far window of her room was a second bed. In it was a child whose face she couldn't see. *Another patient*, she thought. *I've never had a roommate before.* A medical chart rested on the dresser between them, and Tabetha reached over and grabbed it. She read the name at the top:

Thomas M.

And this story might end here if not for what happened next. For Tabetha was about to make one last discovery. As she glanced across the room, her eyes caught upon something and so halted at the bedside of her roommate. He had a small wooden box. Just big enough for a pen.

Hmmm, Tabetha whispered, a strange excitement growing within her. *I wonder if he likes to write too . . .*

Part Two

Author's Note

I do not think you would like my library. It is dark and dusty, and in the winter quite cold. The stones of the floor are uneven in places, and the walls, which would scowl if they could, give the unfriendly feel of a dungeon. But above all, it is not a safe place to read. My collection I consider quite dangerous.

Dangerous? you ask. *What could be more harmless than a book?*

But a book, I tell you, is as a blade! It may not pierce armor or splinter a shield—yet words, those ideas captured in·ink, will cut when improperly handled.

My library holds some ten thousand tales, and I have copied each one by hand. Every book is therefore dear to me, as I'm sure you understand. Yet I have often fantasized that should a flood—or even worse, a fire—have its way with my collection, and were I forced to rescue only what could be carried in these arms, I would not hesitate in my selection.

My steady hand would reach for the highest shelf and draw from it a single tale.

Bound in yellow twine.

My name is The Karakul.

Tabetha saw a strawberry-colored birthmark, shaped distinctly like the sun.

*N*ow I should begin Part Two by reminding you this story moves rather quickly, and it assumes you have already shared some of Tabetha's journey; that you have met her strange friends and gazed wide-eyed upon the empire of Wrush; that you have known astonishment to the bottom of your boots. It assumes you have already wept tears of laughter and those of sorrow, too, and perhaps even trembled with a good deal of fear. That you have gasped when she gasped, cringed when she cringed, cheered and thrown kisses, turned somersaults of excitement and then cackled like a madman as you pitched your hat at the sun, waving both hands in the air and screaming wordless lunatic cries of unbelievable joy and freedom while galloping wildly and recklessly through the white-hot flaming pages of Part One!

If you have not, do so.

I am an old man now with little enough time as it is, and far too cranky to muck about with its retelling.

So! Let us continue this tale. I draw your attention back to the old city hospital, to a small, lonely room with a small, lonely bed beside a small, very lonely window on a cold day toward the end of September.

It was raining. Tabetha hummed to herself as she watched tiny droplets slither down the window. In her mind it was a race they held, each droplet speeding toward the bottom of the glass. Tabetha touched one raindrop, tracing its path with her finger. The drop wiggled its way down, starting and stopping, starting and stopping, growing ever closer to the window's sill. But then her raindrop's path met another and unexpectedly sidetracked. It took a different path entirely, and Tabetha's little droplet never finished the race at all.

Tabetha turned from the rain-spattered glass to the sound of rustling sheets across the room. It was Thomas M., her new roommate, who lay across his bed scribbling intently into his spiral ring notebook. The boy's hair was so black it reflected white in direct light, reminding Tabetha of the sheen on crow feathers. But she had seen this boy's moods too were of a color with crows. Thomas was a very troubled child. It had been a week now since Tabetha's return from Wrush, and not once had she been able to make him smile.

She sometimes wondered if stories of her adventure might cheer him up. He never had to know they were true. But something stopped her each time she began to speak, and her magical journey remained hers alone.

Soon, she decided with a jolt of excitement. Very soon now, Tabetha would take out her magic pen. She would write her way back to the empire of Wrush.

A frustrated snort rose from across the room.

"What are you writing?" Tabetha asked Thomas, but at the sound of her voice, the boy rolled onto his side with a grunt, turning his back to her as usual. Tabetha pushed up higher, trying to glimpse the stories he was always working on. Like her, it seemed, Thomas loved to write. He could write all day, even into the night, but making friends didn't interest him in the least.

"How about if we trade wheelchairs for the day," Tabetha suggested. "I've done it before, and we could even race!" But Thomas just curled tighter into his sheets, the scratch of his pen on paper filling the silence.

He wasn't ill like her. Thomas had been in an accident. Still, he couldn't walk any better than Tabetha, and he would probably be in the hospital just as long. She couldn't understand why he refused to talk to her.

"If you change your mind, just let me know," Tabetha said as she flopped back against her pillows, lacing her hands behind her head. No matter how hard she tried to understand him, Thomas M. remained a mystery to her.

Tabetha thought back to when she had left the empire of Wrush, and recalled the strange feeling that there was something she could do here, right here in her own world of hospitals and nurses, to help all those friends she'd left behind. What that something was, she didn't yet know. But every time she laid eyes on Thomas M., sullen and gloomy in the bed across from hers, she sensed *he* was the key. That somehow, everything she needed to do in Wrush started right here with him.

Thomas M.

"I almost forgot," Tabetha blurted as she rolled back over to face him. "My mom brought in a whole box of cookies yesterday." Then, in that singsong voice used by little girls with bait, she added, "They're the ones with super big chocolate chi-ips . . ."

She waited for Thomas to perk up. When he didn't, she said simply, "I'll give you one if you want to."

Thomas sat up, turning a scowl upon Tabetha. In his one hand was a pen, which he quickly set down out of view. But on his other hand, Tabetha saw a strawberry-colored birthmark, shaped distinctly like the sun.

"Unless you and your cookies can make me walk again," he said with an icy glare, "then leave me alone." Thomas crinkled the pages of his story into a ball, and she blinked at the hardness in his voice.

"Just leave. Me. Alone."

$\mathcal{L}$

I expect that you, dear reader, will recall from Part One that Tabetha was not one to mope about. It is true, she had on occasion practiced pouting in the mirror, and had watched in awe as other children threw tantrums. But when it came down to it, Tabetha didn't really know how. So naturally, when faced with Thomas and his exotic displays of temper, she was curious and had done her very best to comprehend him. Yet the time had come—he had made it clear—the time had come to leave Thomas be.

Tabetha tugged her private curtains into a tight ring about her bed. She twisted the blinds flat against the window. Immediately the air dimmed and gave the impression of weight. Tabetha stretched sideways as far as she could, reaching, clutching the stack of paper on her wheelchair's seat, then yanked it back onto her lap with a small grunt.

She paused, listening.

Nothing moved.

She searched the long crack where the two curtains met near the foot of her bed, and when absolutely certain of her privacy, Tabetha did one final thing. She slipped a small wooden box from its secret hiding place beneath the mattress and then smiled to herself. She was ready at last. It was time to return to her empire.

Tabetha flipped open the box's lid and removed the magic pen. She began writing, describing images of Wrush. She described the temple ruins in the jungle. The singing river of gold. The giant, who promised to come back one day, his last words still mysterious as ever: *You really need to meet my brother.*

In a flurry of ink and scattered paper, Tabetha described her palace in Etherios, the floating city in the sky. She felt her ceiling open wide above her. She described the Mungling and the

High Wizard of Wrush, and her sheets floated apart like slow clouds. She described her throne lit with bright candles, the white petals of her crown. A breeze brushed her cheek and warmed it.

When Tabetha at last lifted her eyes from the paper, her gaze fell upon a place stranger than dreams.

❧

A field.

Tabetha was sitting in a field, an endless sea of golden grass. Wind rolled like waves through the stalks, and she glanced up, squinted, brought a hand to her brow. The sun roared silently overhead; it boiled and spat with the fury of hot oil. But there was no sound. None at all, except for an otherworldly rushing that filled Tabetha's ears like cool water when she dunked her head in a stream.

Was she dreaming? This place was new and enchanted, yes. It was nothing like Earth. But was it Wrush?

Something deep inside told her *no*.

Tabetha gaped in wonder, watching liquid silver clouds slide across a churning sky. *If not Wrush, then where am I?*

She blinked then, as one does upon waking. In the distance stood an old man.

He raised one arm above the shuddering grass as though waving to her. She tried to call out, to tell him she couldn't walk, but no sound passed the hold of her lips. There was to be, she realized, no talking in this world.

The rushing in Tabetha's ears grew louder. She looked down to her lap. In it was a golden bowl. Then a shadow crossed the sun, and the old man was standing before her. He was tall. Taller than any man she'd seen, with a tangled, long beard and a satchel at his side and robes that hung down to the ground. He pointed to the sun, which was like a frothing coin in the sky, then to the bowl in her lap. The bowl was wide and shallow. It felt warm to the touch. It filled up before her eyes with bright liquid. On its surface showed the image of a map. She understood.

Tabetha lifted the bowl to her lips and sipped deep the elixir. The taste rolled like thunder down her throat, then lightning, and her thoughts glowed as if struck. The sky caught fire and howled.

Tabetha shut her eyes tight. She covered her ears. In her mind she heard a sound like silk tearing. She felt a great rush of wind as she was yanked through the tear, and then nothing. Just silence. Her hands slowly drifted from the sides of her head. She cracked open one eye, then the other, and her breath shook as she stared about her. For it is a shocking thing when the veil between worlds has been torn, and one finds oneself smuggled through the gap.

Tabetha, too astonished to move, gazed dazedly about the empire of Wrush.

His voice alone was
thick with magic.

*I*ndeed, Wrush. Tabetha had arrived, though the manner of her arrival was bewildering. She found herself sitting cross-legged upon the cool tiles of a hall, the throne room of the Citadel. Why, she asked herself, hadn't her pen brought her straight here? Why stop over in that strange world of dreams?

And what, most important of all, had she drunk there?

You see, reader, her magic pen was not the only gateway through worlds. There are many ways. Many. I will not list them all here. What matters is that Tabetha knew two:

Her pen, and whatever she had drunk from that bowl.

She was still feeling shaky and confused when the Mungling burst through a small door at the back of the hall.

"Ahoy there, Tabetha!" he cried out, and she relaxed at once. The Mungling's caterpillar-like face glowed bright with greeting. She was there, she realized, there in her empire, and the Mungling loped across the throne room in an excited circle, just like her dog Pizza always did when she came home from the hospital. "We thought you'd never return!" the Mungling cried as he slid to a halt. Tabetha leaned forward and hugged his soft neck tightly. It had seemed like forever to her, too.

When she straightened, Tabetha breathed deep the clean scent of this place. It was impossible to hold back a smile. "It's great to be back," she said, listening to her voice echo from faraway corners. The Citadel was exactly as she remembered. Nearly empty within, the domes above seemed a mile high and the broad corridors looked just as deep. Thousands of candles flickered in rows beside the throne, repeating themselves endlessly as tiny reflections came ablaze in the walls.

Suddenly Tabetha felt a gush of fresh air, and the candle flames leaned. She turned her head to the mighty doors at the far end of the hall, just as they swung slowly open. Two figures stood there, beneath its broad arch, and Tabetha's heart pounded with joy.

"Hooray! Hello!" she called out, unable to wait for their approach. She lifted both hands and waved.

Her visitors waved back and strode across the hall, politely halting ten paces before her. With his blue tunic, thick beard, and shining helmet and sword, Isaac—the captain of her soldiers—stood broad and strong. "My Lady," he said to Tabetha, a title that still made her look around, "My Lady, how we worried for you! I have not slept a wink since you left!"

"How could he?" joked Answer, the tall boy at his side. "He hasn't bathed either, and the smell of him is enough to wake drunken trolls from their sleep."

Tabetha clapped at that, snickering with glee. But she suspected Answer could just as easily have been lecturing on discipline and his words would have tickled all the same. His voice alone was thick with magic.

She looked at him now, the High Wizard of Wrush, this boy with his coffee-dark skin. He wore only that pair of billowing leather trousers that came short at the knee, apparently unaware that most people wore shirts. Indeed, the wavy script of tattoos that moved up his arms and across his chest in an unbroken line seemed like clothes enough, as if the strange powers within them wove a fabric of their own.

But more than anything, it was that mischievous smile of his that now drew Tabetha's eye, a smile that declared Answer was, unbelievable as it seemed, the protective older brother she had always longed for.

The urge to hug him was overpowering. It was just as well that she remained where she was, for Isaac took off his helmet at that moment and stepped forward. The click of his boots echoed all through the chamber. "I'm afraid you've come just in time, My Lady," the soldier announced. "So much has happened since you left. There's so much to tell! But first things first."

As gentle as can be, Isaac lifted Tabetha from her place beside the Mungling. His huge arms encircled her, then set her tenderly into the seat of the Crystal Throne, saying, "It's only proper that the empress wear this." The giant soldier leaned forward and set a wreath of enchanted white flowers about Tabetha's head. *The Orchid Crown*. The mark of the empress, fashioned from petals that never bruise or spoil.

Tabetha was awash with sensation. She had almost forgotten the thrill of being there in Wrush, with iridescent pigeons cooing in the domes high above and the crystal throne humming at her back. Even in her slippers and blue pajamas, her short brown hair uncombed, Tabetha felt like royalty.

But one look at the fear in Isaac's bearded face and all excitement drained out of her. "What's wrong?" she asked the captain. "What has you so scared?"

The Mungling fidgeted. Isaac cleared his throat. "It's Morlac, My Lady," he said. "The evil sorcerer again. My spies tell me he is up to no good."

"What's he done now?"

"That's the problem," the soldier said. "Nobody knows. But there are rumors of a wild magic afoot. Strange dreams and journeys. All the creatures are aflutter, and I for one believe Morlac is behind it all."

"You think *that's* odd," said Tabetha from her throne. "Before I got here, I was sucked into another world completely!"

The Mungling was aghast as Tabetha described the old man. Isaac's brows crinkled with concern. But it was Answer, the boy-wizard, whose face told it all. He listened closely to her tale, his eyes bright and intent. "I can't believe I'm saying this," he said during a break in her story. "But the man you describe . . . he sounds just like the Stone Tamer."

"The Stone Tamer!" chirped the Mungling. "They say he's the father of all stones, older than Wrush itself!"

"Yes, but there'll be time to discuss that later," said Answer, anxious to hear the rest of the story. "Tabetha must tell us how it ends."

So Tabetha continued, and when she came to the part with the bowl, Answer once again became excited.

"What was in it?" he asked in sudden alarm.

"I don't know exactly," she said. "But it tasted like—"

"You drank from it!"

"I . . . I mean, when the bowl appeared in my lap, I . . ." Tabetha gulped aloud. "Is that bad?"

The wizard fell silent. His eyes went to the golden letters tattooed along one arm. To her surprise, he pinched one between his fingers and lifted it into the air like some sodden leaf that had only just landed. The wizard snapped his wrist as though flicking a sheet, and the golden letter dissolved into sparkles. They glittered for a time, then flexed into an image, a perfect likeness of the bowl with golden cream, now hovering in the air before Tabetha.

"Did it look anything like this?" Answer swept his hand slowly through the image. The fluid rippled, and Tabetha could almost taste its enchanted warmth upon her tongue.

Nervously, she nodded her head.

"What does it mean?" asked Isaac, turning to the boy-wizard.

"It means," Answer replied, still studying the image, "that was no ordinary liquid Tabetha drank."

"Will I be okay?" she asked, her hand going to her belly.

"You need to tell me something, Tabetha. This is important, so try to remember."

"What?" she asked. "Remember what?"

Answer fixed her with his eyes. "Did you see anything resembling a map?"

℘

Good! I believe I have your attention. Now listen closely, as I have little patience for explanations: Wizards, if you have not already guessed, are possessed of extraordinary power, minds clear as glass, and such unbelievable skills as would shatter the brittle walls of your imagination.

Which is very cool.

For instance, by throwing salt on his own shadow, a wizard can fix it in place, a trick of little importance on its own. However, when placed beneath the tongue, that salt transforms a wizard's voice, allowing him to command the very shadows like puppets.

Answer, High Wizard of Wrush, pinched that grain of salt from the floor where it soaked up the shadows, then placed it ever so carefully in his mouth. His lips puckered for a moment as he sucked on the salt, then let his voice sing out like a silken hand, directing the shadows about him. With each strange word Answer spoke, a shadow peeled up from the floor. They changed shape in midair and joined other shadows. Then together they shifted and danced, moving about on the walls, looking for all the world like actors on a stage. Tabetha watched these silhouettes as she would the cast of some play, a mysterious story performed before her eyes.

When Answer finished, all the shadows fell limp. They returned to their owners, leaving Tabetha with a strange understanding.

She had pictures in her mind, things she couldn't describe. Answer had explained to her, through the movement of shadows alone, the legend of an ancient map.

"How old?" she asked.

"*Very* old. Nearly older than words. That's why its story is best told through the shadows, which are older still and have language enough to tell it."

From the movement of these shadows, Tabetha had learned the tale of a map so dangerous it had to be hidden away, locked in a faraway world for safekeeping.

"But if this map were found," the boy-wizard explained, "and someone knew how to use it, the whole universe could be in danger."

"Morlac!" cried Isaac. "Morlac must be searching for the map. And the Stone Tamer wants you to find it first!"

"But the shadows," said the Mungling, throwing a suspicious glance at his own, as if its loyalty were no longer something presumed, "the shadows warned us of pyramids as well. What would pyramids have to do with this map?"

"Pyramids," the boy-wizard replied, "are what this map leads to. Three of them actually, each hidden in a different part of the universe. That's why this map is called the Pyramid Map."

From the look of dread on Isaac's face, Tabetha knew the big soldier had heard of it too. "What do you know, Isaac?" she asked him. "Tell me what you've heard of this Pyramid Map."

And here I must explain a very peculiar trait of Wrush—a feature found in no other world. There is a wind there, both enchanted and rare, that will rise up when a person speaks of times past. It is called The Attar, this wind, and no one can predict when it comes. But since time immemorial, it has perfumed a speaker's words and left the scents of ancient days with those listening.

Isaac was well versed in the legends of Wrush. He approached the throne slowly, going down on one knee. "Long, long ago," he began in a solemn voice, and a sudden sweetness burst upon them, a breeze heavy with spice. The Attar filled the palace chamber like incense, and a drowsy smile enveloped each listener's face, "when Wrush was young, and her children ripe, back when the mountains still sang in chorus and moved about—"

"I'm sorry," Tabetha interrupted, suddenly drunk with the fragrance. "I drifted off for a moment. Did you say the mountains sang?" She yawned. "And moved around?"

"But of course, My Lady," the captain replied. "Though not on legs like yours or mine. Still, the mountains moved about, plowing the earth as they pleased, like great, slow waves of white granite. The ripples of that time can still be seen in the north, where Sun Dogs dig caves in the sky and—"

"Isaac," said the wizard. "The perfume of your words makes us drowsy. If you stray much, and speak long, I fear The Attar will have us snoring at your feet."

"Yes, Wizard," Isaac continued, unabashed. "Well, it happened that one day the mountains of Wrush called all their children to gather. Every rock, stone, and pebble came rolling in. So excited were the little ones to impress their mountain sires that the stones stacked themselves neatly into three towering pyramids. Three pyramids, My Lady, from the first days of our world. Three *Guardians*, we call them now, though they have been hidden so long, no one but the map remembers where."

Three pyramids, thought Tabetha, quickly perking with interest. "But why call them Guardians?" she asked. "What do the pyramids guard?"

"Legend tells us," said the captain, "that the magic of the Three Guardians alone divides our world from yours, and yours from ours. The pyramids' magic makes up the wall between these worlds. Like a great, enchanted fence that keeps them safely apart."

Tabetha imagined a magical force field, an electric blue net stretching from one pyramid to the next, separating Wrush from her own world.

Then she saw it crumbling.

"So this is what Morlac plans to do?" she asked. "To break down the wall between worlds?"

"It appears so," Isaac grunted, a shadow crossing his broad face. "But to do that he must first find each of the three pyramids."

"And to do *that*," added the wizard, "he'll need to find the Pyramid Map. For as soon as it's in his hands, the magic of the pyramids can be destroyed. Without the wall between worlds, there would be nothing to keep Morlac and his army of Gwybies from marching straight to your Earth. With no one expecting him, he would conquer all in a day."

Tabetha felt a shiver run down her spine. Never did she expect her *own* world to be in danger. Certainly Earth had its problems: There was sickness and war, hunger and hate, and even the forests and the oceans were menaced, but so far as Tabetha knew, evil sorcerers had never posed a genuine threat.

Now, like a burr in her mind, images of Morlac and his Gwybies clung fast to her thoughts. She saw his creatures spreading like ants, sprinting loose over hills and pouring down through the valleys until all the Earth fell black with their shadows. Suddenly her chest felt tight, as if a huge stone lay upon it. Her palms slicked with sweat and tingled. She was terrified, for she was the Empress of Wrush and if the boy-wizard was right, only she could stop Morlac and his army.

She took a deep breath and calmed herself, thinking it through one last time.

"Then we'll just have to find the Pyramid Map before him," she said in a voice wobbly with newfound determination.

The Mungling let out a cheer. "I knew we could count on her! I knew it!"

Answer raised his hand and the Mungling fell quiet. "The Pyramid Map could be anywhere, Tabetha. We have no idea where."

This was true, Tabetha knew, and it made for no small predicament. She had no idea how to even begin seeking the map.
For a moment, Tabetha considered her family back home and
what they would make of her journeys. She wondered what her
father would say if he knew that his daughter had been yanked
between worlds and now had an army of her own, or that she
was ever on the lookout for Gwybies. Then, for some reason,
she thought of Thomas M., that strange angry boy with a birthmark like a sun. She wondered if they could ever make peace.

Tabetha startled, realizing someone was talking to her. It
was Isaac, and he looked more worried than ever. "I beg you,
My Lady," the captain was pleading. "Please don't go searching
for the Pyramid Map. Many people have tried, yet none have
returned. Seeking the Pyramid Map is simply too dangerous."

Of course, you can imagine why a young girl might hesitate.
Isaac was not advising against climbing on shelves or touching
dead birds or licking jelly from the end of a knife. He was talking about danger. *Real danger*, and when brave soldiers, heavy
with armor, furrow their brows with concern, it is considered
wise to listen closely and with care.

And Tabetha knew this. She knew she was just a child. She
knew the Mungling carried her because she couldn't walk on
her own and that she needed her medicine every day at noon.
She was not a knight or a wizard, or even especially brave. In
fact, she was frail and fearful, and even a little homesick at
times. Yet only one response came to mind.

"I have to," she told Isaac. "I have to try."

The huge soldier shook his head. "Please, My Lady. As your captain, let me take your army out to meet Morlac and his monsters. We will defeat them on the field of battle and then—"

"No," Tabetha said in a voice quiet but strong. The hall fell silent, and even Tabetha felt surprised by the courage in her words. "No, Isaac, I'm sorry. Though I don't understand it, something deep inside tells me *no*. Battle is not the way."

And even as she said this, she knew there would be a battle. But not now. Not yet. "I have to go," she said. "I have to find the Pyramid Map before Morlac does. And I need someone to stay here, someone strong, to stay behind and guard the people while we're gone. Will you do it, Isaac? Will you stay?"

Answer stepped to her side. Tabetha looked from the shining boy to the Mungling. They would help her, she knew. They would follow her to the end.

"Something deep inside tells you *no*?" Isaac blurted, his beard wagging in bewilderment. "But that makes no sense! And where will you go?" he asked as the Mungling helped Tabetha into the saddle on his back. "How will you even know where to begin?"

Answer squeezed Tabetha's feet into the stirrups. He took her by the hand, and together with the Mungling they started for the palace gates. "I'll just follow my heart," Tabetha called back over her shoulder to Isaac, "for as long as it keeps saying *yes*."

"The memory feels a thousand years old."

You might be interested to know there are more than sixteen different species of head lice in Wrush. But the one most cherished, and thus shared between loved ones, has a chirp like a cricket, only more melodic, so that each night at sundown as the teafires are stoked, whole quarters of Etherios break into song. As you can imagine, a household without its own chirping lice is considered a dismal, dirty place, and unnatural, too, as it is tradition for a family to sing harmonies before supper.

Once outside the palace, it was the cheerful hum of these creatures that drew Tabetha's attention, and she searched the crowds with both ears and eyes to discover the music's source. Answer led her and the Mungling across the courtyard, where flowering vines whispered along high marble walls and the townsfolk sang ancient whale songs. Ninety-nine kites were cut free, acrobats drank fire, and children scampered across rooftops tossing blue spice in the air. "The empress!" they shouted. "The empress has returned!"

Amid this strange music and pageantry, Answer halted at the edge of a gaping hole, right there in the middle of the courtyard's sparkling tiles. The hole was perhaps ten feet across and set about with plush carpets. Tabetha peered down through the gap and saw the ground far below.

Very far below. The tiny green specks, she suspected, were trees. Only then did she recall that she was high in the sky, the floating city of Etherios dangling like a swing beneath the Cloud Shepherd and his flocks of Cloud Sheep, bound there by invisible cords.

Tabetha tipped her chin up into the blue and the Cloud Shepherd smiled back, but slowly, the way clouds always do, his mouth breaking apart and gently coming together in a grin. His flocks covered the sky in great woolly lumps, but the mountains Tabetha remembered were nowhere to be seen. The city must have floated elsewhere since her last visit.

A great bundle of sticks and rope lay piled beside the hole's carpeted edge. "Be careful on your way down," said the wizard as he gave the bundle a shove with the heel of his bare foot. It was a rope ladder, and it tumbled over the edge, unraveling like a long, wobbly tongue. Its fall whispered into the distance and then went silent, with only the hiss of wind to replace it. Moments later, the ropes jerked tight against the hole's edge.

The ladder had finally reached the ground. Its bottom end was so far away, it appeared thin as thread swaying against gusts of whistling breeze.

Tabetha gulped from atop the Mungling's back. She didn't remember the climb being quite so high on her last visit.

"Great view, isn't it?" the Mungling tittered. "I love it when the Cloud Shepherd picks up speed." The sun-wyrm dipped his head down through the hole, and his face rumpled in the wind. "Whew!" he called excitedly when he lifted it again. "Invigorating! Shall we give it a go?"

Before Tabetha could reply, the Mungling began backing down the ladder. Tabetha wrapped her arms about his neck for dear life. "Eck!" he said with a choking sound. "Not. So. Tight. Please!"

Reluctantly, Tabetha relaxed her grip, but she pinched her eyes tight. The wind screamed through her hair and bit at her cheeks; her whole body flung sideways when it gusted. She felt her stomach lurch, certain she would be peeled from the Mungling at any moment and cast to the ground far below. "I feel like we're on a spider's web in a hurricane!" she squealed.

"Yes, yes!" cried the Mungling. "Isn't it great?"

Tabetha forced her eyes open. The ground was nearing. The trees now appeared bigger than her feet. But to the east, as far as she could see, stubborn hills rolled to the horizon. These hills were bald and rocky, wretched with emptiness. Not a tree could be found. What's worse, Tabetha saw what appeared to be giant rib bones thrusting up from the hills. They reached for the sky like broken, bleached rainbows.

Turning her head, she found a very different sort of scene. To the west was a river, banked with green orchards and a village of thatched rooftops. A friendly path wandered between the cottages, packed with horses and carts and people in colorful clothes. Tabetha saw children eating apples on the rooftops.

"Aha!" cried the Mungling as he landed on the ground with all six legs. "Was that incredible or what?"

Tabetha was too relieved to reply. Instead she studied the rope ladder, watching it jiggle as Answer fearlessly descended, drifting slowly north with the wind.

She glanced at her wristwatch. Ten o'clock in the morning. That left only two hours till noon, when the nurses came into her room each day with medicine. Her medicine was too important to miss. Tabetha did want to get better—to walk again without a Mungling or a wheelchair, to run in the sun and feel warm grass beneath her feet . . .

I *sure don't want to be late,* she whispered to herself as she set the alarm on her wristwatch. She began pressing tiny buttons with her fingernail.

But that leaves only two hours to find the Pyramid Map! she thought, then recalled with relief that time moved much slower in Wrush. Two hours on her wristwatch could equal two days in the empire. She had plenty of time—she hoped. Tabetha heard the watch beep six times, which told her the alarm was ready.

"There. Now I won't forget when it's time to go."

As Tabetha finished, she heard the soft thump of bare feet slapping earth. She looked up and found Answer smiling back at her, perhaps thirty yards away. His curvy-lettered tattoos glistened in the sun. As he strode toward her, he glanced casually from the river-village on their left to the treeless hills on their right. His overall manner was relaxed, cheerful—a mood Tabetha would have liked to share.

"So which way now?" he asked when he arrived. Tabetha looked for a long while in one direction, then the other. Between her two choices, the village certainly looked more inviting.

"Well," Tabetha said a little uncertainly, "I told Isaac I would just follow my heart."

"What does your heart say now?" asked the boy-wizard.

It was a simple question. But when it came down to it, Tabetha's heart said lots of things.

"I'm not too sure," she confessed. "The hills look so barren and harsh. Not like any place I'd like to travel. But . . ." She sighed. "I guess I'm a little confused."

The wizard stepped near, that brotherly grin returning to his face. His ink-dark eyes twinkled as he scratched the Mungling behind the ear. "You know what I do when I'm feeling unsure about something?"

Tabetha shook her head.

"I dive deep inside, and listen to the quietest voice I can find." He smiled. "Eight hundred years now, and it hasn't steered me wrong yet."

&

As you may be thinking, reader, eight hundred years is an unusually ripe age for a young boy. Very few, these days, make it much past twelve or thirteen. But Answer, High Wizard of Wrush, was not like other children, and for this reason Tabetha took him quite seriously.

The quietest voice I can find . . .

The wizard's words played freely through her mind, for some reason calling up images of a moth, alone, small and bright, winging its way through moonlit meadows. It was a beautiful image, the sort only a wizard's words could create. Tabetha was inspired, and she decided to give it a try.

The quietest voice I can find . . .

She closed her eyes, expecting silence. What she found instead was more like a dozen radios in her head, each turned up full blast, each crackling for the whole of her attention.

The first voice was useless, a skipping CD: I *don't know,* I *don't know,* I *don't know,* it repeated, while a second voice insisted she avoid those horrid hills.

A third voice agreed, pointing out how friendly the village looked, and a fourth sang a song from a commercial.

Tabetha's mind was a parade of distractions, a carnival of thoughts, all fluttering about like confetti. Each voice added something new and colorful. Yet none took her to that quietest place inside, that place where all was still and the right choice lit up like the sun between clouds.

"I can't hear it," she told the boy-wizard, chewing her lip in frustration. "I'm really trying, but there's so much chatter in my head. I just can't find that quietest voice."

The wizard said nothing in return. He simply gazed out toward the Bone Hills.

Tabetha sighed. She itched the side of her neck. She straightened a crease in her pajamas. She lifted the flat of her hand to shield the sun, which was violet at midday. The Bone Hills, however, glimmered gold with noontide heat. And as she watched, the smallest something stirred deep within her. Not quite a voice, but it tugged all the same. Excited, she listened closely.

Then it faded like a breeze, drowned out by the chorus of louder thoughts.

Answer turned his dark eyes to her own. "Have you chosen, then?" He pushed up from his seat, brushing his hands together as he stood. "Will it be the Bone Hills or the river-village?"

Tabetha clicked her tongue in indecision. "I think maybe . . . the hills?" she said with a wince, wishing she felt more certain. If only that tugging had been stronger or had just told her what to do. Why couldn't she hear the quietest voice within? In a moment of despair, Tabetha wondered if perhaps she didn't have one.

"Oh, yes, yes, the hills," chimed the Mungling. "As good as anywhere, I suppose, when we really don't know where we're headed. Unless you have a better idea, that is." He cocked his chin at the boy-wizard.

Answer just shook his head. "Of the three of us here, only Tabetha has seen the Pyramid Map, which makes her more an expert than me. If the empress says 'To the hills,' then to the hills we go."

But something in the wizard's expression gave her pause. "What is it, Answer? What aren't you telling us?"

The eight-hundred-year-old boy just looked up at the sky, as if reading banners no one else could see. He turned his dark gaze to the rolling mounds. "The Bone Hills," he said, nodding. "They can be safe at times."

"And at other times?" she asked, following his eyes across the desolate folds of rock and bone.

Answer puckered his lips; they squeaked with dismay. "Treacherous," he said. "Sleep Storms are common this time of year. Very common, especially this far south. I've seen them sweep down out of nowhere, faster than hate, and swallow up whole caravans with their elephants and all. Most people don't even bother to run."

"Sleep Storms can . . . kill you?" Tabetha asked hesitantly.

"No," said the wizard. "Though they may as well. No one ever wakes from a Sleep Storm." He took a sip from a waterskin. "We do have one thing going for us, though."

"At least there's that!" said the Mungling, ever joyful and ready for adventure.

"The Stone Tamer was seen in these hills not long ago," said the wizard, passing the waterskin to Tabetha. "If we're lucky, we might bump into him."

Before long, the three friends were deep in the Bone Hills, cresting knoll after barren knoll. The sun burned hot. Even the Mungling was sweating. Answer led the way, picking a path between rocks and the tremendous rib cage of some long-dead beast. Tabetha watched, fascinated, as Answer's sorcerous power twirled the dust of his footprints into tiny cyclones. Within moments, she realized, his every print had vanished, leaving no trace of the wizard's passing.

"So what kind of creatures were these anyway?" Tabetha asked as they passed close enough for her to pat a great white rib. Her eyes followed its curve high into the sky, but the sun swallowed its tip and nearly blinded her. She glanced quickly down again, blinking yellow spots from her vision.

Answer stooped to pick up something colorful, cracked it between his fingers, and popped it in his mouth. "They were called Pump Dragons," he said as he chewed. "But they're long gone. These ones here must have starved." He ran a desert-dark hand along the side of an enormous femur, the long bone from the upper part of a leg.

"They must have been huge," Tabetha commented. Each rib was as big around as an oak tree. Their shadows stretched like colossal, curving stripes across the burning land.

"They had to be huge," replied the wizard, "to drag the mountains as they did. Pump Dragons wore great harnesses made of silver and were like giant oxen on a yoke. How else did you think the mountains got around?"

"Well, I don't know," said Tabetha. "The mountains where I come from all stay put."

Answer scooped up another object. A shell, she realized. He was picking up iridescent shells. He cracked this one, too, and popped its contents into his mouth. "It's the same with these mountains now," the wizard said, pointing into the distance with the shell in his hand. "Without the Pump Dragons, the mountains' roots have grown deep. But there was a time when the mountains wandered, when the people knew them by name and threw festivals when their favorite peaks passed by."

For some reason that made Tabetha sad. She had never even heard of Pump Dragons before, yet suddenly she felt their loss from this world. "What would it take to bring the dragons back?" she asked, wondering if it might be as simple as inviting them.

"They won't be coming back," said the wizard. "Not for a long, long time. Their food's all gone."

"The Noble Fruit was their favorite," the Mungling added.

The wizard spread his arms to include all the Bone Hills. "But as you can see, there's nothing but rocks here now. Rocks and bones. After Morlac created the Gwybies, the first thing they did was cut down all the Noble Trees in the empire."

"What happened then?"

"The Pump Dragons settled for Peace Fruit. When those were cut down, too, they were left to scrabble for Restless Fruit and Grumpy Fruit—even the odd bit of Greedy Fruit—none of which ever agreed with them."

"They found the Angry Fruit unbearable," said the Mungling, "and only a few Pump Dragons could stomach the Boring Fruit."

"By that time," said the wizard in a sad voice, "the only edible food left to them was the Shy Fruit. After eating that, the Pump Dragons dove deep into the ground, never to be seen again."

It was at this point in their journey that something peculiar took place. Tabetha could not have explained it if she'd tried. The Mungling turned to her, and as she gazed back at him, she saw the reflection of a dragon's rib cage in his eyes. Instantly, Tabetha recalled a certain dream—a dream that you, dear reader, may remember from Part One. It was a strange dream filled with blue flowers on a hill, and for just a moment, for the tiniest flash in time, that dream came to life before her eyes. Instead of Pump Dragons' bones, it was the blue hill Tabetha saw, even the rutted old field with the tangled fence-line. She gasped in surprise, and then it was gone. Vanished like a reflection in the window.

What was that all about, Tabetha asked herself, left with a strange, pressing feeling that the Pump Dragons of old and the blue hill from her dream were somehow, in some impossible way, connected. This was made all the more strange by a single fact: The Pump Dragons were from Wrush, while the blue hill was a real place on Earth, a place near her parents' home. Why she had dreamed of it, again and again, Tabetha could not begin to guess, and its link to the Pump Dragons was an even greater puzzle.

"Well, it sure would be nice to see one," Tabetha said at last, still sorting out the images in her mind. "A real live Pump Dragon, I mean. It just seems so sad that they're all gone." Then she remembered something else. "And it can't be right, but I even have a memory of riding one once."

"A Pump Dragon?"

"Yes. It makes no sense. I don't know when it could have happened, though the memory feels a thousand years old. But I used to think about it a lot, especially when I was younger. One time I even told my dad."

"And what did he say?"

"It was a dream. He said it was just a dream, and that sometimes even adults get confused between old memories and dreams. Kind of funny, huh?"

Answer nodded, walking in silence for a time. At last he paused to pick up another iridescent shell. This one he handed to her. "Pepper Slugs," he said, showing her how to crack it open. "About the only thing worth eating in these hills."

Tabetha wrinkled her nose at the tiny creature. It was slimy, and she wasn't very hungry. But considering the rapturous look on the Mungling's face as he chewed, she decided it might be worth a try.

"Wow," she said, her little teeth grinding and grinding. "They're kind of tough. And spicy. Like old gum, but on fire."

"Great for spitting long distances, too. Watch." And then Answer launched a great gob of spit as though it were a golf ball slapped with a four iron. "Give it a try," he said, and she did, but failed miserably. The spit just trickled down her chin. She laughed at herself, and the others joined in.

"No, it's like this," Answer said, trying to keep a straight face. He helped her along in her new skill, feeding her slug after slug until she got it right. Sometimes Answer seemed so much like an older brother, Tabetha forgot this was the High Wizard of Wrush, the most powerful sorcerer in the empire, teaching her how to spit without dribbling.

"I think you've got it now," said the wizard at last with that familiar, mischievous smile. "The whole empire, I'm sure, is a safer place for having an empress who can spit straight as a camel."

The boy-wizard trekked ahead, and the Mungling turned back to Tabetha in her saddle. He dropped a handful of the colorful shells into her pajama pocket. "You should try the dried ones boiled in a tea some time!" he said in an excited whisper. "Drink two cups and you'll pee every color under the rainbow!"

Tabetha laughed. "Really?"

"Really!" the wizard called from far up the trail. How he had heard their whispers from up there, she would never know. And she had no time to wonder, for her attention was immediately drawn elsewhere. The landscape was changing. Along with huge bones, there were now odd stacks of boulders, some the size of small towers. They balanced in great teetering columns so tall Tabetha couldn't imagine how they had gotten there. The Mungling called them Hoo Doos and told her they grew up from the ground like anything else.

But even stranger to her was what Answer did next.

"Why are you covering one eye?" she asked, for he walked along using the palm of one hand like an eye-patch.

"Lots of Wink Holes in these parts," he said. "They're almost as dangerous as the Sleep Storms."

"Should I cover an eye too?" she asked.

"If you want to see a Wink Hole you should, and it might be best. You don't want to fall in."

Just then, the boy-wizard came to a halt. He gestured for Tabetha and the Mungling to do the same. Tabetha looked around. As far as she could tell, Answer was standing atop a rocky rise, no different from any other. The distance remained crowded with Hoo Doos, dragons' bones, and endless sweeps of golden hills. The only difference was the smell. The air here seemed hotter, drier, and carried the faint scent of gasoline, a smell Tabetha was for some reason always fond of.

"See what I mean?" the wizard asked after a pause.

"No," said Tabetha, feeling confused. "I don't see at all what you—"

She gasped, having lifted one hand to her eye. Her jaw clenched tight in surprise.

Yes, she nodded slowly to herself. Yes, I *know* exactly *what you mean*.

"Anything to make the empress smile."

*S*till winking, Tabetha gazed down into a pit so big, so black and deep, it looked able to swallow Etherios with room to spare. The entire thing simply appeared out of nowhere the moment she shut one eye. "How did *that* get there?" she asked in amazement.

"From the Pump Dragons!" chirped the Mungling, peeking over the rim of the crater. "Left over from when they cast off their harnesses and dove. These Wink Holes are all that remain."

Tabetha studied the giant black tunnel in wonder. "How deep does it go?"

The wizard picked up a pebble. He tossed it into the hole. "All the way," he said. Tabetha strained to hear the pebble's fall, but she heard not a sound, as if the tunnel had no bottom.

"What do you mean, 'all the way'?" she asked. "All the way where? Where do these tunnels go?"

"Other worlds. Other places." Then Answer glanced at her. "See why you don't want to fall in?"

Tabetha nodded, unable to peel her eyes from the Wink Hole. "Other worlds . . . ," she whispered to herself. Then: "So there's lots of them. I mean, Wrush and Earth aren't the only worlds?"

Answer tossed another pebble into the hole. "There are worlds beyond number, Tabetha, all through the universe, and every world has a Wink Hole into it. Every world, that is, but one."

"Which world is that?"

The boy-wizard met her gaze. "Yours," he said. "Of all the known worlds, only Earth has never known the tunnels of a Pump Dragon."

⁊

The sun was setting blue across the shoulders of the Bone Hills. The shadows grew long, and a chill lifted goose bumps from Tabetha's pale skin. Yet still, she couldn't pull her eyes from the bottomless black of that Wink Hole. A *Pump Dragon made this,* she kept telling herself. A *Pump Dragon, digging tunnels between worlds.* She wondered which world lay at the end of this one, and if the dragons ever found their Noble Trees. Then she thought of the pyramids' magic force field, and how it kept the Pump Dragons from finding Earth.

"Have you ever heard the word *exclude*?" the wizard asked her.

"Sure," said Tabetha. "It means when you're left out."

Answer chuckled. "That's right. Being excluded doesn't feel very nice. But in this case, it's a form of protection. Earth, for very good reasons, was excluded long ago from the dangers and unpredictability of our universe."

Earth, Answer told her, wasn't exactly the center of the universe, but it was dear all the same. Earth, he told her, was *the universe's heart.* Just like the one in her body, it was a thing the universe couldn't do without. For a moment, Tabetha wondered what Earth would be like if the pyramids' magic force field ever did come down and the Pump Dragons dug their way in. At first, the thought excited her. She imagined all the wonders of Wrush splashing through the tunnels, washing over Earth like nectar.

Then she recalled Morlac, the sorcerer, and his monstrous army of Gwybies. *They would come too,* she remembered, and fretted that the heart of the universe, Earth, could ever fall into Morlac's evil hands.

"It will be dark soon," said the wizard as he stepped back from the pit, pulling a shawl from the Mungling's saddlebag and setting it around Tabetha's shoulders. His eyes went to the Hoo Doos as if searching for shelter. "Wink Holes will be hard to see at night. It won't be safe to walk."

Tabetha glanced at her watch in the fading light. Eleven o'clock.

Only one Earth-hour left to find the Pyramid Map, she thought, chewing her lip with concern. Would she find it before she needed to return for her medicine?

As the sun disappeared beyond a rumpled horizon, Answer found the enormous half-buried skull of a Pump Dragon with empty eye sockets and long, curving teeth. He called to them and the three friends hunkered together in the hollow of its jaw. Tabetha began to shiver. It would be a long night and most certainly a cold one. The Mungling pressed in close, and to keep their minds off the chill he began telling stories, which of course, "no Mungling can avoid," he was quick to remind her, "for a Mungling's brain sits somewhere just behind the tongue, and it's impossibly tedious trying to divide the two."

He told Tabetha about the Sun Wisps he once saw, who looked like fat little fairies, and whose only job was to grind sunlight into powder. Each evening, he said, when the yellow moon crept out and fetched magic from the shadows, the Sun Wisps would pat their fat bellies and take down their jugs of crushed light. They would laugh themselves inside-out and feed powdered sunbeams to the Blink Fish, who dreamed so hard that baby worlds were born fresh with each dawn.

Answer chuckled at that, and then to Tabetha's delight, he stood to perform a few of his favorite magic tricks. He pulled a hat out of a rabbit and then tied two stones in a knot. Tabetha and the Mungling clapped and cheered, and Answer bowed low, saying, "Anything to make the empress smile."

"My thoughts exactly," chirped the Mungling as he clapped. He wrapped four of his arms around her. "I thought she would never return!" Then he pushed back from her in alarm. "But just look at the poor girl. She's shivering!"

"I do love your spells," Tabetha said to the wizard, trying hard not to show how chilly she was. But the truth was, her pneumonia was at its worst in the cold. Her chest ached to breathe, and it pinched tight when she coughed.

Answer crouched down before her. "Then I have one last enchantment tonight, this one especially for you, Tabetha." He smiled. In the darkness of night, his eyes gleamed with an otherworldly light. He picked her up in his arms like a sleeping babe and carried her out through the dragon's maw. He set her down gently, resting her shoulders against a towering Hoo Doo. Then he took two big steps back, widened his stance, and threw his arms open as though to catch stars.

Immediately Tabetha noticed the tattoos on his arms, all the more dazzling in moonlight. She drew a sharp breath as the script began to move. Answer knitted his fingers together, as though hugging a tree, and suddenly the cursive letters were swimming across his skin. They circled faster and faster, like a ball around the inside of a moving bucket, until they spun free of his arms and whirred in a tight circle above his head. Tabetha heard a fierce whispering as the golden letters lifted high into the night. Then silence fell as they disappeared.

A quiet moment of sadness.

"They're gone," Tabetha said to the sky.

"Not to worry," replied the wizard, sitting himself down on a rock. "They'll be back."

No sooner had he said this than a distant clamor filled the air. A warm breeze swept a lock of hair into Tabetha's eyes. As she pushed it back, she saw a moth, small and fluttering, with wings like glass coins shot through with the sun. It came to rest on her shoulder and she beamed with pleasure. The little moth pumped its wings open and closed a few times, then Tabetha's eyes flew wide in amazement. She brought a finger to its wing, where tiny veins of red light beat to life, pulsing and throbbing, pulsing and throbbing. To Tabetha's surprise, she felt a tiny pin-prick, and her shoulder flooded with warmth.

"An Ember Moth," said the wizard with a satisfied grin. "It's sure to keep you cozier than blankets."

Just then, something golden streaked through the air—many golden somethings, in fact. They were Answer's tattoos, she realized. They had returned. Tabetha looked one way and they swooped from the other, making another mad dive past the wizard. His tattoos seemed to be enjoying themselves, the blurring tails of light they left tracing through the air. At last the golden letters settled above Answer, whispering quietly to one another before alighting on his arms and chest like a flock of pet birds.

Immediately following, the night itself began to quiver. A great shadow slid free from the sky. Tabetha strained her eyes, peering into the gloom, quite certain the shadow was taking a new shape.

"What—" She swallowed, sitting forward with interest. "What is that huge thing in the sky?"

A word to the wise.

When throwing rocks at a hive swollen with killer bees, there are just a few things to bear in mind. First, though it may seem obvious, make certain to use your strongest arm. This will allow you to stand as far away as possible, thus giving you the greatest chance of escape before they catch and sting you.

Second, do not jump into a lake or other body of water, as the bees will likely be waiting for you when you come up. Instead seek shelter, or run through tall weeds. This will offer some cover.

Swatting, a very ancient technique still in use today, should in fact be your last resort and used only if you wish to die by stinging. Keep in mind, however, that bee colonies often leave their nests in spring and fall in search of new hives, a phenomenon known as *swarming*. When swarming, killer bees have no hive to defend, and so they are unlikely to sting at this time.

This is not true of the Ember Moth.

The Ember Moth, though Tabetha did not know it, is a venomous, swarming insect, much like the bee. The main difference is that the sting of the bee hurts, whereas that of the Ember Moth does not. Its harmless venom is well known to cause heat.

Tabetha squinted, a broad grin on her face, as a trembling cloud of Ember Moths fluttered down from the sky, pouring down around her like rain. Their clamor was immense. They rushed and they thronged, their wings beating the dark air. Tabetha covered her face with her hands and giggled as they spilled all about, tickling her ears, tussling her hair. The air throbbed with countless webs of red light.

Within moments, Tabetha and her friends were covered from head to toe in a pulsating cloak of electric wings. Her chest relaxed and she found it easier to breathe. Looking at the Mungling, Tabetha could see only his big eyes all aglow, and she stifled a laugh for fear of scaring the moths away. She gave instead a long sigh of contentment, letting their warmth wash over her like a steaming-hot bath on a cold winter's day.

But as she relaxed, so too did an uneasiness stir deep within. The tiniest hint of something prickled the back of her mind, like a thing forgotten that she should have remembered, or something important that only she could do. When Tabetha opened her eyes, trying to discover the source of her agitation, she found herself staring directly into the gloom of the Wink Hole.

This frightened her a little, and even though her eyes couldn't quite pick out the black of the Wink Hole from the black of night, she could *feel* it. As real as wind or bone or the heat of the Ember Moths, Tabetha could *feel* that bottomless pit tugging at her heart, drawing her near as if by the end of a rope. What was this strange calling that led her into the Bone Hills? And now this even stronger pull to the Wink Hole?

Tabetha was about to describe this odd feeling aloud when all of a sudden, her teeth clamped in alarm. A sound, like footsteps approaching, brought the wizard upright and sent his blanket of moths skittering into the night.

"Mungling!" Answer hissed, his expression alert. "Quickly! Get Tabetha into your saddle. Then hide, if you can." His eyes searched the gloom. "Whoever approaches has no fear of the night." Then Answer shot them both a look of warning. "That in itself is cause for fear."

$\mathcal{L}_{l}$

The footsteps grew louder—and closer. Tabetha heard the distinct sound of small pebbles crunching underfoot, then of someone breathing, loud and slow, as they trudged up the nearest slope. Whoever it was headed straight for their camp.

"There's no time, Tabetha! Hurry!" whispered the Mungling as he flapped his many hands in a panic. "Get on! Get on!"

Grunting loudly, Tabetha hoisted herself up to the Mungling's saddle, but her pajamas got caught in a stirrup. "Hurry!" cried the Mungling, shoving at her feet, but her leg wouldn't come free. She grabbed her leg and tugged, yanking with all her might. She opened her mouth to yell for help, and then quite suddenly, her whole body was overcome with a strange calm, thick as molasses. Her muscles relaxed. Her arms went slack. A large halo of light floated into the camp, and all the panic drained from her like black water down a twirling spout.

"The Stone Tamer!" declared the wizard in awe, and Tabetha realized that indeed, it was a man approaching, a delicious glow of soft light encircling him. The Stone Tamer was nearly ten feet tall with a robe of grey wool and tiny bird's nests tucked in the long tangles of his beard. A leather satchel was slung over one shoulder, and as he strode along, humming deep notes, he reached into his bag with a gnarled old hand and withdrew fistfuls of sparkling powder. These he flung upon the Hoo Doos he passed, which began to grow before Tabetha's very eyes.

Answer, the Mungling, and Tabetha crowded together in a knot. The Stone Tamer came straight for them, his stride long and slow, his eyes fixed on the sky above as if seeing only the stars.

"I don't think he's noticed us," said Tabetha, her curiosity growing with each crunch of his footsteps.

"Impossible," spouted the Mungling. "He's only a few steps away. Surely he—"

But the Mungling wasn't able to finish, for the three friends were forced apart as the giant old man strode between them.

And passed, without so much as a nod.

Tabetha and her friends turned in amazement. The Stone Tamer's humming grew faint as he receded into the night, the glow of his halo slowly dimming.

"That was a little odd," commented the Mungling as they watched the Stone Tamer go. "I'd always heard he was a strange fellow, but that was too much. It was as if we didn't even exist." He sighed. "Oh well. Perhaps it's for the best. You never know with these weird folks from legend. Which is why we Munglings have a saying: 'Never trust a—'"

"Hey!" Tabetha shouted at the old man's back, surprising the Mungling and the wizard both. "Hey, you! Hold on!"

The Stone Tamer halted, as did his humming. He turned to face them with an ominous air.

"Uh-oh," said the Mungling, taking a nervous step backward. "Perhaps you shouldn't shout like that, Tabetha."

But strange as it was, Tabetha felt no fear. Why this was so, she couldn't yet say. It was just another of those extraordinary moments when something took hold deep inside her, and she found herself doing things she scarcely believed possible.

"Stone Tamer!" she shouted across the distance. "I have a question for you!"

And little did she know at the time, but the answer that followed would change her life—and many other lives, too—forever.

"A hundred of your lives is but the flicker of my eye."

A wise man once pointed out that if you watch closely at just the right time, you will notice that babies are born with their hands clenched in a fist. It is as though they grab hold of life, and everything in it, during that very first moment on Earth.

Yet you may also observe, if you are there at just the right time, how we die with our hands open and empty. This may seem a small thing at first. A trivial matter. Until you consider the lesson hidden in our hands:

All that we hold, we let go of in the end. Nothing we cling to is kept.

As you will soon see, Tabetha too must let go, and she would not find what she needed till she did.

Tabetha felt the Mungling tense beneath her as the Stone Tamer, slow as fog across water, drifted toward them over the barren slope. "I hope you know what you're doing, Tabetha," chattered the Mungling as the old man drew near.

She turned to the wizard, who met her gaze with a faint nod, assuring her that he would not leave her side.

Yet once again, shocking even the wizard, the Stone Tamer ambled right past them all. He strode off the way he had come, flinging sparkles of dust at the columns of stone. Never once did he look in their direction.

"Wait a minute!" cried Tabetha, and urged the Mungling into the light of the old man's halo. Answer was beside her in a flash, and the three of them stood before the Stone Tamer, looking up into a face so old that years alone could not measure it. He appeared to be studying a Hoo Doo behind and above them, watching it grow with grave satisfaction.

"Down here!" Tabetha said, waving her arms, and the old man swiveled his great head, appearing startled to see them at last.

"My, my," his voice rumbled, deep and thick. His lips smacked a few times as if these words were rare food and his full attention were required to savor it. "Now, let's see if I can name you all before you disappear. You, I shall call a Driddler," he said, pointing to the Mungling. Knobby old fingers combed through the knots in his beard. "And you," he said, addressing Tabetha and Answer with a nod of his shaggy chin, "shall be known as Bumble Slumps. And all your kind are free to call me Old Man Shale, if you please. Or just the Stone Tamer, as most generally do."

Tabetha and Answer shared a look of confusion.

"But we already have names, sir," she said, then cleared her throat. "Mine is Tabetha Bright, and my kind are called *people*."

The Stone Tamer just smacked his lips open and closed, perhaps tasting this thought, and said finally, "Very well. People you shall be." Then he started off again into the night, humming softly.

"Wait!" Tabetha shouted. When he stopped, she said to his back, "Don't you remember me? I saw you in a dream."

He said nothing at first, his back still to them. "Then it was your dream," he said. "Not mine."

"You really don't remember?"

He said nothing. Hesitantly, Tabetha added, "I thought . . . It just seemed like . . ." She stopped. Maybe it had been just a dream. "I wanted to ask if you'd help us."

"Of course you did!" he said as he spun, surprisingly quick. "But as you can see, I am quite busy now. All the mountains need growing, and these seedlings here are in need of my care." He pointed to the Hoo Doos.

Baby mountains, she realized with a smirk. The Bone Hills were nothing but a mountain nursery.

Unsure what to say next, Tabetha simply asked, "Why did you call us Bumble Slumps? Have you never seen people before?"

Old Man Shale thought for a long time, and Tabetha wondered if he might have fallen asleep standing up. At last he said, "You must be new here. You . . . *people*, as you say. Or else I would have met such creatures before."

"But people have lived in Wrush for thousands of years," voiced the wizard.

"My point exactly!" replied the Stone Tamer. "I, myself, have been around for millions. Anything younger than a volcano or a sea has to do a lot of hand-flapping and hey!-shouting before I stop to notice. A hundred of your lives is but the flicker of my eye. You'll find none more ancient than myself. Now, if you'll excuse me, I have the rest of the world to attend to."

Once again, he made to leave, but Tabetha pulled the Mungling up in front of him. "If it's truly Wrush you care about, then you'll want to hear what I have to say."

A tiny bird chirped and burst from a nest in the Stone Tamer's beard. "Is that so?" he replied.

Tabetha chewed her lip. This was her last chance. If the old man didn't listen now, he never would. In a single breath she said, "Scattered somewhere across the universe are three pyramids whose magic forms an enchanted wall that protects Earth from the Pump Dragon's tunnels."

"Of course, of course," he said impatiently, waving a hand as though she had described to him last week's news. "The *Hedge* is nothing new. Certainly nothing to get up about. So what of it?" he asked.

"The Hedge, sir? I don't know what you mean."

"The *enchanted wall* you speak of, child. It's been called the Hedge since before my first chin whiskers grew."

"Well," Tabetha continued, "The map to those pyramids may not be as safely hidden as you thought, and an evil sorcerer named Morlac plans to find that map, seek out the Three Guardians, and tear down the enchanted wa—that Hedge, sir . . . as you called it." She paused, expecting to see surprise or even alarm in the old man's face. Instead she found only the deep, steady eyes of one who had seen all things come and go in his time.

"Don't you understand?" she cried. "If the Hedge comes down, the Pump Dragons will dig tunnels to Earth in search of food. There'll be nothing to stop Morlac from bringing his armies through those tunnels and conquering the heart of the universe!"

Old Man Shale let out a long, slow exhale, fluffing out the dense hair that covered his mouth. When he spoke, his tone was not unkind. "Such things happen," he muttered. "Worlds are born. Worlds pass. New and wild creatures run amuck. For myself, I prefer my gardening. I'll stick to my mountains and stones if you please, which are more easily tamed than your whims."

Tabetha slumped in her saddle. The Stone Tamer wasn't going to help her after all. Sadly, she tugged on the reins, wheeling the Mungling about. She started off, head hung low, when suddenly, she became aware of something like a fist in her heart—a hand. A little hand, opening up, just enough to let the sadness through. She felt a sweetness, then a soft warmth in her chest. And immediately, miraculously, as though in response, the Stone Tamer called out from behind:

"Did I mention I collect trinkets?"

Tabetha paused, uncertain. Slowly, she turned and shook her head.

"Oh, yes, you know the kind," he continued. "Mostly charms and such. A few fancy gems. Been gathering them about me for years. There was one in here just today, I believe. I know

I saw it—or was that last year? Humph. Either way. Now, let's see." Old Man Shale hummed to himself as he rummaged deep in his satchel. After a moment, he withdrew a small leather sack, knotted at the top with eel whiskers. He came forward and slipped the sack into Tabetha's hands. She felt several small pebbles rolling about within.

"What are these?"

He knelt close and looked straight into her eyes. "Thunderdrops!"

She looked again at the small sack. Whatever was inside, they felt nothing like thunder. "What will I do with them?"

The Stone Tamer feigned a look of surprise. "You mean, you don't know?" He grumbled to himself while lifting the flap of his satchel, pulling the mouth wide so she could see.

Darkness.

Bottomless black inside.

"Would you like a hint?" he asked, his eyes twinkling with amusement.

Tabetha smiled, nodding. He bounced his eyebrows playfully and then gestured for Tabetha to peek once more into his satchel.

And that was the last thing she remembered—the Stone Tamer bouncing his eyebrows—before she peered within. Then only the flash of stars and burning comets as she tumbled headlong into the depths of space.

So many stars . . .

Tabetha lost count as she fell through the universe, casting about without hope of return. She could almost feel the endless black of space against her skin—cool and soft, like swinging with her eyes closed. Every now and then, a planet hurled past or a distant star warmed the curve of her cheek. Otherwise she floated endlessly, as if in a dream, uncertain where she was headed or how long till she would get there.

At some point—after an hour or a year—Tabetha found herself nearing the very edge of the universe. The stars grew dimmer, the blackness more thick. The silence was so loud she heard it sucking at her ears. Yet she tumbled on, her skin all a-tingle, to a place that should have been the very end all things.

But in her heart, she knew it was only the *beginning*.

ℇ

Confused?

No harm in that, for it will give you, I believe, a rather small taste of Tabetha's journey. Yet for all her headlong tumbling, nothing made Tabetha so dizzy as her abrupt return to Wrush.

Perhaps if you, dear reader, had ever been unexpectedly jerked into the magical depths of the Stone Tamer's satchel, cast among stars on an impossible voyage, only to be rudely awakened by an indescribable stench, flat on your back in the Bone Hills of Wrush with the cold of night prickling your skin, you might better appreciate how Tabetha felt upon waking—or returning, I should say—from her most magnificent passage through the universe with Old Man Shale.

"I wouldn't try that," were the first words she heard, somewhat jumbled in her ears, spoken by the boy-wizard to the Mungling. "The empress might not appreciate squished stink-beetles up her nose."

So that's the smell. Tabetha's eyes were still shut, and were in fact very hard to open. She felt movement against her hair and realized she was lying down with the wizard cradling her head in his lap.

"No, no! No harm intended!" she heard the Mungling say. "I only thought to help. Mother Munglings always say beetle guts up the nose is the very best way to wake a lazy youth."

"I don't think she's lazy," the boy-wizard replied, dripping cool water across Tabetha's tongue. "I think Old Man Shale just took her on a little tour. A *very big* little tour, if I had to guess."

Tabetha coughed on the water and forced herself upright. "Where is he?" she asked, looking around. "Where's the Stone Tamer?"

Answer pointed into the night, and she saw the tip of the old man's haloed head, just as he descended a stony slope. "But where's he going? He didn't even explain!"

"Who knows?" said the Mungling with a shrug. "Wherever he came from, I suppose. You never can tell with that sort."

"Tell me what happened," said the wizard in a kind voice. "Maybe I can help."

So Tabetha told them of all she'd seen. She told them how she'd been sucked out into the universe, traveling forever and a day. She told them about how time had slowed, and of the extraordinary feel of open space against skin. She told of the stars and the planets, and of blackness thicker than tar.

Then she told them of the *beginning*.

"Hmmm," grumbled the wizard with a nod. "This *beginning*, you say, was at the very end of all things? Beyond the edge of the universe?"

Tabetha nodded.

"What was it like?"

"Well," she began, "at first it was like nothing. No sounds. No colors. Not even a thought in my head. Then out of nowhere appeared a lagoon, an enchanted lagoon. Its water was the brightest turquoise you ever saw. I saw huge glass towers climbing straight from its depths, and in the very center of the lagoon was a tiny island. More like a grassy mound, really. At the top of the mound was a well."

"A well!" said the wizard with a look of concern.

"Uh-huh. A wishing well. There was a fish, too. She lived in the well and she was white as bone, and when she spoke she said, 'There are no endings, Tabetha. Only beginnings in disguise. Now come to me . . .' Again and again she said this. Like I was supposed to remember. And when she disappeared, I saw the image of a map."

"A map!" said the Mungling.

"Yup. A map. The whole thing was pretty weird. I really don't know what to think." She looked at Answer, who appeared deep in thought. Perhaps he had heard of this place, this well. "So what does it mean?" she asked at last.

Answer hesitated. "It means you've found the Pyramid Map," he said. "Or at least you know where it's hidden. This *well* you speak of . . . I know of it, and the Luck Fish, too. I believe it's where the map is hidden."

"But what of the Luck Fish?" asked the Mungling. "Is she some dangerous fiend?"

Answer chuckled. "Not at all. She is said to grant one wish, and only to those who can find her. Her home is known simply as the Beginning Well, as it's the place from which all things come."

"And if Tabetha wishes for the Pyramid Map?"

"Then I think," replied the wizard, "the Luck Fish would have to give it to her."

"Hooray!" chirped the Mungling, glowing with excitement. "We finally know where to go! All we need to do is find this magical wishing well and then Tabetha can ask the Luck Fish for the map."

His voiced trailed when he saw the look on Tabetha's face. His glow dimmed in concern.

And it is here I must pause to tell you something of Tabetha's past.

You see, she was no stranger to wishes. She had made more wishes than she cared to count. Unfortunately, she was no stranger to disappointment, either, as she had learned long ago, and with no lack of tears, that wishing does not make a thing come true.

Tabetha would never forget the first time her father had taken her to the town library. It had been a sunny day, but not too hot. There was a lawn out front where families ate picnics and played, and enormous sycamores spread above the library steps. But it was behind this library, to the marble fountain and its pool, that Tabetha's memories so often strayed.

Tabetha's father, who had been pushing her wheelchair all day, had parked her beside the fountain for a rest. She had peered into the water, where light shifted across the coins at the bottom.

Naturally, she had asked her father for a penny, and upon receiving it had made a wish. But no sooner had she thrown the coin than a second wish had come to mind. Tabetha had asked her father for another.

"Sorry, Tab," he had said, spreading a few coins across his palm. "No more pennies. All I've got left are a few dimes."

"Well, can I have one of those, then?"

Even now, Tabetha remembered how her father had crouched down and the solemn look in his eyes as he'd spoken.

"It's a tough lesson," he had said, "but you may as well learn it now. Life certainly won't keep it secret for long."

"What do you mean?" she had asked, noticing as his hand closed on the dimes.

"What I mean is this." Her father had stood slowly and slipped the coins back into his pocket. His gaze had fallen upon the sunny surface of the water. "No wish is worth more than a penny."

From that moment on, Tabetha had built a wall against wishes. She kept them bolted in the basement of her heart. Wishes brought pain when they didn't come true, and she had more than enough pain in her young life already.

"Tabetha?" asked the Mungling. "What's wrong? Didn't you hear what Answer said?"

She nodded.

"He says all it takes is one wish. We're only a wish away!"

She nodded again.

"Then why so sad, Tabetha?" The Mungling furrowed his brows. "You look like you've been told to drink poison."

"I know," said Tabetha. "It's hard to explain."

This may have been true for her, in that moment at least, but in fact her difficulty was really quite simple. Tabetha feared failure and disappointing her friends. She feared disappointing herself, the world, and everything in it, by putting all trust in a wish—the one thing she had decided never to trust again.

A wind had started up. Answer climbed to his feet. "Before you get too excited," he said to the Mungling. "I should remind you—it's not that easy. This Beginning Well, it's not in Wrush. It exists in another world entirely."

The wind grew stronger, and Tabetha felt a twinge in her gut.

"A world called Haza Mugad. Even if we could get to this world—and I'm not at all sure that we could—we would still need to find the Lost City where the well is hidden."

The Mungling sighed, covering his face with two of his hands. "I should have known. This is terrible. Terrible! Tabetha finally figures out where the Pyramid Map is, and now we've no way to get there. I've never even heard of this Lost City of Haza Mugad! Are you absolutely certain that's where the Beginning Well is hidden?"

Tabetha didn't hear the wizard's reply, for something unusual had caught the corner of her eye. It was hard to make out at first; it looked like a cloud of black smoke boiling in the distance. But as it rolled across the hills, kicking dust into the sky, understanding flickered through her mind. A warm breeze whispered across her cheek. Then all at once, a howling gust of wind whipped the hair from her face.

"It can't be!" cried the Mungling, squinting in the wind.

"But it is!" shouted the wizard above the din. He lifted Tabetha into her saddle. "A Sleep Storm is upon us! Quickly now! Follow me, or even tomorrow will be nothing but a dream!"

Something deep inside told her different.

*A*nswer rushed Tabetha and the Mungling down the steep side of one hill and between the Hoo Doos of another. Tabetha heard the Mungling panting beneath the rising din of the storm. Already it was nearer, louder, a ravenous shadow clawing at her back. The crisp smell of it was thick in her nose, and the dark sky above crackled with power. She glanced ahead, in the direction Answer now led them. Endless hills lay that way, as far as the eye could see.

Tabetha cranked her head around, peering over her shoulder into the approaching storm. She saw faces taking shape, swirling and raging like explosions of black flour. She gasped as one face formed an evil grin, looking directly at her.

"This way!" she heard the wizard cry as they raced along the rim of a Wink Hole. "Careful along the edges! Careful now, or you're sure to fall in!"

But Tabetha could see this was hopeless. The Sleep Storm was too big, too fast, too near for them to escape, and the Bone Hills seemed endless as the stars. Any moment now it would swallow them whole. Tabetha covered one eye and peered into the bottomless pit beside her. The Wink Hole was a gaping mouth into the unknown. Answer had told her to avoid it, to never go in.

Something deep inside told her different.

Like that gentlest tug that had first led Tabetha into the Bone Hills, something pulled at the very bottom of her heart. She suddenly understood that while it was all right to be afraid, fear didn't change what she must do.

Tabetha gulped. She understood, all right. Because beneath it all, she had always known what had to be done. Ever since she had first stared into its depths . . .

"This isn't the way," she said to her friends, and something in her voice caught them like hooks. The wizard paused. He turned to study her face.

"There's only one escape from the Sleep Storm," she said. She urged the Mungling to the very edge of the Wink Hole so she could gaze into its murk, and then glanced into the wizard's eyes.

"Down," she said, and threw herself from the saddle into bottomless black.

$\mathcal{L}$

Of her passage through the Wink Hole, Tabetha recalled very little. It seemed to take all of forever, and only the blink of an eye. She had the funny feeling she was going down a long, slippery slide, with countless turns and loops in a tunnel black as night. She heard the yelps of the Mungling somewhere far behind. Then came a blast of light, a flood of heat, and Tabetha felt herself lifting, sucked high into the air as if through a whale's spout, before falling again. She landed with a thud in the warm sand of a giant red dune.

Tabetha looked up, dazed and disoriented. Seven suns burned white overhead. Clouds hung low and churned like steam. As far as she could see, there were dunes—red dunes, wrinkling a desert so big and hot, her eyes ached against the bitter brightness.

Moments later, Tabetha heard the Mungling's yelps grow louder, then saw him squirt straight into the sky as if on the tip of a geyser. He landed with a soft *thunk!* nearby, laughing good-naturedly and rubbing all six of his shoulders.

"Now that was a ride!" he exclaimed, then turned to the sound of a muffled cry. *Answer*, Tabetha thought, and then the boy-wizard was tossed carelessly into the air. His limbs skittered about like an insect held by its wings, until they lost sight of him beyond the crest of a nearby dune.

"Come on!" the Mungling chirped as he gathered Tabetha atop his saddle. Together, they rushed to the wizard's aid. When they found Answer he was already standing calmly, brushing sand from the faded creases in his leather trousers. His dark eyes searched the desert, and then raised to take in the suns above. The look on his face worried Tabetha.

"What is it?" she asked. "Do you know where we are?"

The boy-wizard shook his head lightly in amazement. "You're not going to believe this," he said, "but this is the world of Haza Mugad. I can tell by the suns and the way the sand smells like ground spice." He let a red handful run through his fingers.

He is right, Tabetha realized. The sand was spicy in her nose and seemed to lighten her thoughts. She could hear the soft buzzing of sunlight, and saw the flash of heat lightning in the distance.

"If this is Haza Mugad," she said, "that means the Beginning Well is somewhere nearby."

"The Pyramid Map too!" chirped the Mungling, his smiling lips rusty with sand. "You never cease to amaze me, Tabetha. Honestly. Nobody else would have jumped into a Wink Hole. Not even the High Wizard of Wrush."

"But he did jump," Tabetha reminded him. "And so did you."

"Yes, yes, of course! But only because the empress jumped first," he replied, flashing her a look of adoration. "How do you do it, Tabetha? How do you always know the right thing to do?"

"What do you mean?" she asked.

"I mean the Wink Hole. How did you know to jump?"

Tabetha frowned, not quite certain herself. "I don't know," she said with a shrug. Mostly she couldn't believe she'd jumped at all.

"Was it that gentlest voice?" asked the boy-wizard. "From deep down inside?"

Tabetha didn't think so. She had felt something pull, yes, and it had come from deep inside. But it wasn't a voice.

"It was different," she said. "I didn't actually hear anything. I just . . . I just knew what we had to do."

Answer smiled and gave her that mischievous grin, and Tabetha—as if from that gesture alone—felt the distinct sensation of something untwisting in her mind. It was completely unexpected, like looking into a mirror and discovering all at once that she wore pearls. "Are you saying that was it?" she asked. "That *pull* was the quietest voice?"

The wizard arched an eyebrow as though repeating her question.

"But I thought there would be words," she said, "words I could hear, and my mind was just too loud to find them."

"Or maybe," said the wizard, "you've been listening all along."

Answer closed his eyes, and Tabetha suddenly saw herself back in Etherios. As had happened before, Answer inserted images into her mind. She realized now it had been the quietest voice that had guided her when she had asked Isaac to stay behind, the quietest voice that had insisted she search for the Pyramid Map.

It was the same when she decided to enter the Bone Hills, and then again at the edge of the Wink Hole. Each time she had been listening to something deep, deep inside, though that quietest voice was never quite what she had expected.

"I guess the quietest voice doesn't always speak with words," she said. "Sometimes there's nothing there but a knowing."

Answer beamed with pride. "You've got it, Tabetha. You've finally got it. *Knowing* is that voice, the one you thought you couldn't hear and yet followed as naturally as water travels downhill. Even when we can't hear the words our hearts speak through the noise, we *know* them."

Tabetha was delighted. What an incredible relief to know she had such a voice! And she was all the more pleased to learn she had been listening.

And if things had gone differently, Tabetha might have said this aloud. She might have thanked Answer for a wizard's wise teaching. She might have told him she was a better person at his side, and that he always made her feel safe. She might have told the Mungling he was her very best friend. As it was, she said none of this. Nor had she even the breath to speak.

A familiar roar erupted at their backs and blasted red sand a mile into the sky. Tabetha's whole body jolted at the sound. Answer lost his footing and fell. Tabetha turned, her jaw dropping in shock. "It's so close," she whimpered, as its shadow rose up like a cliff. *So much closer than before . . .*

This time, she knew, there would be no escaping the Sleep Storm.

ℛ

No one, not even the High Wizard of Wrush, could have predicted such a thing. Never had it been seen before. And yet there it was, the Sleep Storm; it had followed them through the Wink Hole with all the determination of hounds.

Wind whipped the clouds into long, smoky streaks, blotting out the suns like curtains. The Sleep Storm's howl was deafening, yet Answer's voice, like a porpoise leaping from sea, somehow rose above it with water-slick grace. "You must go now," he said to his friends, his tone eerie with calm. Over his shoulder Tabetha saw a wall, a tower of sand and smoke, a great blackness rushing straight toward them.

"The wizard is right, Tabetha!" the Mungling shouted anxiously. "Trust him! He knows what he's doing! Now quickly, we must go!"

Tabetha's throat thickened, and she was too terrified to breathe. Her eyes darted about in a panic. Answer was leaving her! And there was no time to think!

"No!" she cried, reaching for the wizard. "I know you're brave! I know you want to protect me, but even you aren't powerful enough to stop this!"

Yet Answer was already leaving. He took a step backward toward the storm. There was a strange peace in his eyes, though his expression was sad, and just as he turned from her, just before sprinting into the gale, Tabetha heard him whisper two words:

I *know*.

＆

The Mungling kicked up little clouds of sand as he raced Tabetha away from the storm. The wind approached hurricane force, lashing at her back with a vengeance. Atop the high crest of a dune, Tabetha yanked on the Mungling's reins. He stopped short and wheeled around to face the storm. Immediately they were met with a blast of hot air that nearly threw Tabetha back as it whipped her cheeks red and forced her eyes into slits.

She could see the Sleep Storm from here. It was like a tidal wave of darkness boiling down from the sky, and the wizard below seemed so small in that moment, arms outstretched before his doom. It put her in mind of the tiniest butterfly trying to hold back a flood. So beautiful, yet hopeless.

Not so different from a wish.

Her eyes misted over, and she heard the Mungling gasp. And then it was over. He was gone. The Sleep Storm crashed over her wizard, her friend, her brother, and Tabetha shut her eyes.

In her grief, Tabetha vowed to keep them closed forever. She would not open her eyes, and she would not save the empire. *What's the point?* she thought. There was no escape. She ignored the Mungling's pleas and the swift rising of the wind. Even through closed lids she watched as darkness swept across the suns. She heard the storm pounding far dunes, then swallowing those closer. Its rage was volcanic.

Then a great rush filled her ears, and the sting of sand was against her cheeks. But she thought only of Answer and did not open her eyes.

She felt the Mungling lifted high, felt herself ripped clean from the saddle. But she thought only of Answer and did not open her eyes.

The bellows of doom crashed all around her; the storm gripped her tight in its fist. Swirling and tumbling, crashing and roaring, Tabetha flailed in the din. She squeezed her eyes tighter and hugged her arms for dear life—until, without warning, all the noise slipped away and a sweet quiet filled her mind like winter sun. For a brief instant, she forgot about Answer.

She thought only of sleep, and amid the slumber of ages, Tabetha Bright opened her eyes.

"I won't lie to you, Tabetha. Things are not good."

*A*m I *dreaming again?* Tabetha asked herself as her vision tumbled across golden fields. A frothing sun burned bright above, and there was no sign of the Sleep Storm.

I *am sleeping,* she realized, running her hand over the tall grass. *The Sleep Storm has me, and now I will dream forever.*

Tabetha let herself fall back in the grass. She stared up at the sky. As her eyes drank in the strange light, she was struck by the familiarity of this place, this dream. In a flash, Tabetha knew where she was. She opened her mouth to call out for the Stone Tamer, but no sound came forth.

Silence.

Just as before.

There was only the soft buzz of sunlight as it dazzled over the bright prairie. Tabetha lifted her head to gaze upon a faraway ridge. It stood all alone, like an island at sea. Atop it, Tabetha saw something move. A person, perhaps. Tabetha blinked and was suddenly there, with no memory of crossing the distance between.

She found herself sitting cross-legged in the sway of tall, golden grass. Across from her, the old man did the same. She peered at him in wonder. His face was wrinkled as an old apple in the sun, and his beard twisted down into his lap. His eyes were soft, and newborn-clear.

"You seek the *beginning*?" the Stone Tamer said without speaking.

"I seek the map," Tabetha replied in just the same way, for in this place words were not spoken but felt only.

The old man nodded, his eyes twinkling bright. "The Pyramid Map is near," he said. "But first you must wake."

Tabetha gazed around her, at the eerie brightness of this world. "I can't," she said. "No one rises from the Sleep Storm's spell."

The Stone Tamer held forth a wide golden bowl. He repeated slowly, "First you must *wake* . . ."

Tabetha peered into the bowl's creamy depths. She saw shapes within, mixing and tossing. She took the wide bowl in both hands. She lifted it to her lips.

She drank.

Delicious warmth rolled to the ends of her fingers. Her mind emptied of all but one question.

"*What . . . is . . . it . . . ?*"

With dreamlike slowness, the old man's lips shaped silent words. She heard nothing. His voice thundered in her head.

"DREAM BUTTER!"

ℒ

Have you, my dear reader, ever watched a dog sleep, and then heard it bark aloud at strangers in its dream? A funny thing, that. It's as though the dog were in two places at once, both dreaming and awake. And the dog will never know this was so.

Of course, we do not bark at strangers or even loved ones when we sleep, and yet we people may not be so very different. My point is this: There are many worlds, and it is in our nature to browse.

Though we may not always know that we do it.

"You're awake!" gasped the boy-wizard, rushing to Tabetha's side. "But that's impossible!"

Tabetha pushed herself upright, blinking the sleep from her eyes. Looking about, she found herself on the floor of a golden bubble, a magical sphere nestled safely in the very center of the Sleep Storm that swarmed around it. Breathing sharply in surprise, she realized she'd escaped the spell. And Answer was *real*.

"You're alive!" she cried, throwing her arms about him. "But how did you survive the storm?"

Answer gave a half-grin and pointed to the bubble. She realized his arms and chest were not glistening with those cursive letters. "Your tattoos made this magical sphere?" she asked, and he nodded.

Outside, the storm raged all around them. It slithered across the bubble's walls, as silent and thick as dark water viewed through the windows of a submarine.

Tabetha remembered the Mungling.

"The Mungling!" she whispered. "Did he . . . is he . . ."

"Of course not!" came the Mungling's familiar chirp from behind her. She twisted around and found his chubby, caterpillar-like face glowing bright with excitement. "I suppose I could have mentioned it before," he said, "but we Munglings don't sleep."

"Never?"

He shook his head. "Pretty hard when you're born to nests in the sun." Tabetha smiled, recalling that Munglings were in fact from Earth, were those odd flecks of light squirming about in the sky, and that she had made a promise to help him find his name one day.

"Well, I'm very glad for you both," she said, hugging them tight. "I never expected to see either of you again."

"We thought you would sleep for a billion years," said the Mungling. "How did you ever wake?"

She paused. "I don't know," she said with a look of startled confusion. "Though I feel like I should know. It's so strange. All I can remember is that I dreamed."

And this was true, for Tabetha did not recall drinking the Dream Butter—but of course, you and I remember how it happened. We know it was the butter alone that carried her through a door between worlds, the butter that broke the spell of the Sleep Storm.

Tabetha would remember this in time, but alas, not yet. The wizard was no less impressed. "All I can say"—he shook his head in amazement—"is that it must have been some dream you had, Tabetha. I've never heard of anyone escaping a Sleep Spell."

"But it was so much more!" she said. "It was like . . ." She broke off in frustration. "I just wish I could remember. There was so much. So many things."

"Things?"

"You know," she said, "things I did and said. And things I heard, too, only it's all slipping away so fast. There is one part I remember, though." Her eyes lost their focus as she recalled the old man's words. "I think the Pyramid Map is very close."

She looked outside, beyond the translucent walls of their magical bubble. The storm wrapped itself about them like smoky grey gauze, but it appeared to be breaking up, little by little. She caught brief glimpses of sunlight through gaps in the churning cloud.

Tabetha glanced at her wristwatch. Eleven-thirty. That left only thirty Earth-minutes to find the Pyramid Map and return to the hospital for her medicine. At the thought of home, she suddenly recalled Thomas M., alone and melancholy in his bed by the window. Would he like her more if she told him of her adventures among distant worlds? Would he be happier and want to be her friend?

Then Tabetha thought of Isaac, the captain of her soldiers. She wondered if he was well, and if he was still brooding over her request that he stay behind. She hoped he wasn't. But more important, she hoped Isaac had managed to keep Etherios safe from Morlac's Gwybies.

Slowly, the sky began to clear. The clouds hung low as steam once again, and Tabetha at last wondered what lay beyond this red desert. *The beginning*, she told herself, but she had no idea what that meant. Was it just a wishing well, or was it something more?

"Mungling," she said. "How do you suppose I'm meant to find the beginning? How should I even *begin*?"

"Hmmm," he grumbled, rubbing his soft chin as he thought. "Well, I imagine it's rather hard to begin, until of course you get started. And even harder to stop if you haven't. But in truth, we Munglings have never done well with such questions. We generally start everything at the end. And just stay there."

"Thanks," said Tabetha, who was not quite sure why she smiled. She patted his head, then a little scratch behind the ears.

Suddenly she was impatient to begin. "Do you think it's clear enough to leave the bubble?" she asked.

For reply, the wizard whistled sharply through his teeth. The walls of the bubble began to tremble, and peering beyond them was like looking through waves of heat. As the bubble began to fade, Answer's tattoos became visible. She saw tiny golden letters whirring slower and slower. At last they halted, molding themselves onto the boy's dark skin. The bubble was no more, and the surrounding landscape left Tabetha in awe.

"Oh, dear," whispered the Mungling, clearly shocked by the scenery. "This is *not* what I remember leaving behind."

Tabetha turned frightened eyes to the boy-wizard. "Where has the desert gone?"

"The storm must have carried us away," he replied, putting both hands on his hips. "That's all. Not to worry." Despite his smile, Tabetha thought it was he who looked most worried. *When the High Wizard of Wrush worries,* she thought, *something is terribly wrong.*

Answer exhaled loudly, and Tabetha followed his gaze. Instead of spice-red dunes, she saw only fields of grey ash. The whole landscape appeared scorched and smoldering. Except for one object. Or one kind of object, of which there were many.

"What are those?" Tabetha asked, pointing to the countless giant eggs scattered across the hot ashes.

"Oh, dear," the Mungling said again.

"Oh, dear is right." The boy-wizard rubbed at his jaw. "I won't lie to you, Tabetha. Things are not good." He paused, clicking his tongue in dismay. "We're in the dead center of a Lightning Field."

ℒ

Now if you, dear reader, wish to know how Tabetha felt in that moment, surrounded by countless eggs of unhatched lightning, simply imagine yourself standing on ice. That's right. Now imagine this ice is not thick, but in fact like the skin of a grape, and beneath it lies only the cold depths of the sea. Naturally, you would not wish to move, for fear of the dreadful events sure to follow. Yet remaining still is no better, as there is danger in the place where you stand.

Now imagine these things alongside a great need for hurry, and the ever-more-urgent need to go pee, and when all this is fixed in your mind, you will have some idea, I believe, of what it was like for Tabetha, stranded among the smoldering ashes of a Lightning Field on the faraway world of Haza Mugad.

Tabetha, at any rate, was not pleased. "Do you think any of them are ready to hatch?" she asked with a gulp.

"It's hard to say," the wizard muttered as he crept from one lightning egg to the next. "I just don't know much about these things, least of all what wakes a bolt of lightning from its shell. Perhaps it's just loud sounds we need to be careful of."

"How loud?" asked the Mungling, pressing his ear to the side of a shiny white egg.

Answer tugged him back. "Anything louder than a dragon's burp, I would imagine."

Tabetha frowned. "I'm not at all sure how loud that would be." She fumbled nervously with the handful of Pepper Slugs in her pajama pocket, not liking their predicament in the least. The egg nearest her flashed from within, and she leaned back in alarm. The egg took on a red glow and then flashed again. It looked like a whole storm had been caged within each fragile shell.

"Not to worry, Tabetha." The wizard forced a smile. "As long as we're quiet, no eggs are likely to blow." Tabetha, however, wasn't so sure about that. In a quick movement, Answer lifted Tabetha up onto the Mungling's saddle. She patted the sun-wyrm's neck beneath her. "It'll be all right," she said aloud, more to still her own trembling than anything else.

They began their slow march, quiet as can be. It was like treading through a field of bombs, with each egg just waiting to go off at the slightest sound. The heat of the ashes brought sweat to Tabetha's brow, and the Mungling's steps sent clouds of grey flake aflutter.

If she strained her eyes, Tabetha could just make out the shimmer of a faraway ridge to the north. She breathed a sigh of relief. The Lightning Field didn't go on forever. "I think we should head that way," she said, pointing to the ridge. But her eyes were turned south in order to see the wizard as she spoke, and beyond him, a most terrible sight caught her eye.

"Oh, no," she whispered.

The wizard turned to follow her line of sight. He shook his head in frustration. "If it's not one thing, it's another," he sighed. "Mungling!" And the sun-wyrm rushed to his side. "Whatever happens, don't stop for me this time. Take the empress due north. Toward that ridge." Over the wizard's shoulder, spread out across the horizon, Tabetha saw the wink and twinkle of a thousand spear tips flashing in the sun. An entire army was approaching from behind.

Gwybies . . .

"Could Morlac and his monsters have come through the Wink Hole, too?" she asked, feeling knots of fear yank tight in her belly.

The wizard nodded, feeding a pouch-strap through the buckle on the Mungling's saddlebag. "Sure looks like it." He tugged down, and the strap made a cinching noise. "Morlac is searching for the Pyramid Map too, after all. It was only a matter of time before we crossed paths."

"We'll just have to hurry," said Tabetha, trying to hide the fear in her voice. "If we hurry, we can get to the map first."

Answer shook his head. "No one can outrun Gwybies over flat land." He tugged another strap tight. "They're way too quick."

"Then what do you plan to do?" asked the Mungling.

The boy-wizard paused, staring blankly at the saddlebag. "I don't know yet." He turned to face the Gwybies, sucking his lips anxiously as he thought.

Tabetha began trembling anew. She reached deep into her pocket, thinking to grab hold of the shells, something, anything to still the nervous tingle in her skin. Instead of finding shells, however, her fingers curled comfortably around a small leather sack. The Stone Tamer's sack. Her whole body relaxed. She withdrew the sack, staring at it with awe and realization.

"I might have an idea," she said, slowly holding forth the Stone Tamer's gift.

"Terrific!" chirped the Mungling, cheerful as a hundred birds on a line. To the wizard he said, "I've learned that few things are more exciting than one of Tabetha's ideas. I've survived several now, and I can assure you, each and every one is absolutely dangerous!"

Tabetha pulled the drawstring on the sack, feeling the eel-whisker knot come free. She tipped the bag into her palm. Out spilled a dozen glittering red gems.

"Thunderdrops," she told them.

"What is it you're thinking?"

She turned to the boy-wizard. She held up a gem. "I'm thinking a dragon's burps can't be any louder than thunder."

But first
you must wake . . .

*B*ack on Earth, usually in early spring, it sometimes happened that a shadow would pass swiftly over the sun. Looking up, Tabetha would find birds, hundreds if not thousands of them, flying so close together that when they cut a sharp turn, they appeared to be a single creature. A single mind.

Presently, watching the Gwybies charge toward her over the fields of grey ash, Tabetha understood something in that moment. Something rather important about Morlac's army.

Whatever it is that allows a flock of birds to move as one, to think as one, Gwybies didn't have it.

Nor was grace, of any kind, part of their tactics. Instead they teemed. They stumbled. They bumped and fell wrestling. They trampled those fallen, then shrieked and pressed on with all the quiet elegance of a sack of bowling balls thumping down stairs. Yet they were fast, those Gwybies, and already frighteningly close. Tabetha clearly saw the twisting horns on their heads, their long, hairy legs. Something about the movement of their tails made her gag.

"Well," the wizard announced, "I have no better ideas. If the empress says Thunderdrops, then Thunderdrops it is. Just tell us what you need us to do, Tabetha. We're all yours."

"Bury one of these gems in the ashes beside an egg," she explained. "As the Thunderdrops heat up . . ."

"*Kaboom!*" said the Mungling, clapping his hands with glee. "Thunder should certainly be loud enough to hatch an egg or two. What a show it will be!"

"The lightning should slow Morlac and his Gwybies long enough for our escape," Answer added. He placed a Thunderdrop exactly as Tabetha told him. He covered it with a blanket of warm ashes and patted it tight. "That should do it," he said. "Now what?"

Tabetha urged the Mungling forward, in the direction of the ridge. "Just keep planting them as we go," she said, clinging to her courage like a cloak in a downpour. If she was right, the Gwybies' lack of discipline would have them retreating from the lightning, with the ranks of their army tangled in knots.

Answer planted another red gem. Then two more after that. "They don't seem to be working," he said, looking back nervously over his shoulder. "And the Gwybies are getting closer, Tabetha. Much closer. Perhaps I should—"

CRACK!

The first of the Thunderdrops exploded far behind them, and a jagged shard of light ripped through the sky. Tabetha heard the shrieks and cries of Gwybies scattering in fear. Clouds of grey ash lifted in the chaos.

CRACK!

A second Thunderdrop blew. Twin bolts of lightning clawed into the clouds, and the Mungling let out a quiet "Hooray!"

"Shhh!" Tabetha warned. "Just keep planting the Thunderdrops. They're our only hope."

CRACK! Another egg hatched somewhere behind. More Gwybies cried out, and in the near distance, Tabetha spied the ridge they sought. It stood out all alone, like an island in the sea. "So familiar," she murmured, a wind of recognition blowing through her.

Tabetha squinted her eyes, peering closer. The ridge's summit was blanketed in tall, golden grass. It pulsed like a tide when the wind blew, and then something stood up. Tabetha's chin jerked in surprise. If she wasn't mistaken, she saw an old man on the hill. An old man with a beard, and a satchel at his side.

But first you must wake . . .

Then the vision was gone, and only the ridge remained, lonely and tall.

"That way," Tabetha said, pointing to the rise.

CRACK! Tabetha turned to find yet another egg hatching, streaks of light splitting a milk-colored sky. The wizard planted the last of the Thunderdrops and rushed to her side.

"Your idea worked, Tabetha. The Gwybies are retreating. They'll have to march all the way around the Lightning Field now."

"We'll have time to find the Pyramid Map after all," said the Mungling.

Tabetha and her friends moved as quickly as possible, slinking between eggs without disturbing a single one. When at last they reached the edge of the Lightning Field, they halted for a quick drink at the base of the ridge. Tabetha found herself gazing up toward the ridge's far crest.

"I know this place," she said, the bits of her dream coming together at last. "This is the golden ridge I saw."

"When?" asked the wizard.

"When the Sleep Storm had me. I know this is it. Even the golden grass is the same." Her eyes danced up the slopes, coming to rest upon the windblown crest. She drew a deep, hopeful breath and then flicked the Mungling's reins. "We'll need to climb it."

The sun-wyrm waded into the tall grasses at once. He huffed his way up at great speed, with Tabetha holding tight and the boy-wizard at their side. After gaining the summit, they paused for a breath. The view was enormous. Gazing south, back the way they'd come, Tabetha observed long fields of ash below. She could even see the broken eggshells of hatched lightning. Answer pointed. She followed his finger. Far in the distance, to one side of the field, she could make out the tiny skirts of dust kicked up by countless feet.

"Morlac and his Gwybies are coming around the side of the Lightning Field," he said. Tabetha wondered how many there were and how long before they would catch up. Then she saw something like a hyena, only bigger and blacker. It carried a rider atop it, skulking along at the head of the troops.

"What's that?" she asked.

The wizard peered closer. "Hinji," he replied.

"What's a Hinji?"

"Largest of the troll-dogs. The most vicious, too. Only one person I know can ride a Hinji like that."

Wishing to see no more, Tabetha twisted in her saddle, gazing north to where the desert resumed. Once again, spice-red dunes pleated the distance like wrinkled sheets. But her interest was not there; it was atop this hill. Tabetha urged the Mungling across its summit, slowly searching through the grasses.

"What exactly are we looking for?" asked the boy-wizard as he helped. "Do you think the Beginning Well is here? Or the Pyramid Map?"

"Butter," said Tabetha, swatting tall, golden weeds aside. "I'm looking for the Dream Butter."

"The what?" Answer was astonished.

"The liquid I drank. Just before I arrived in Wrush. Then again when the Sleep Storm took me. I saw the Stone Tamer, and he told me to find the beginning. But first I'm supposed to—"

Tabetha's eyes came to rest upon a wide golden bowl.

"*Wake,*" she whispered, noting the sunny liquid within.

The bowl was balanced in the depression of a perfectly round stone. The wizard lifted it for inspection. "So this is the stuff, is it?" Excitement was plain in his eyes. "The stuff that carries you through worlds?"

Tabetha nodded.

"Then I suppose some congratulations are in order, Tabetha! This Dream Butter should reveal, once and for all, the secret place where the Pyramid Map is hidden."

The Mungling cheered. "You found it, Tabetha! You found the way to the Beginning Well!"

But what Tabetha was thinking in that moment was not nearly as cheerful. Very soon now, she realized with a sinking feeling inside, she would be asked to make a wish. To welcome failure and the depths of disappointment.

"When we get there," she said in a voice much like a squeak, "when we meet the Luck Fish, I mean, maybe one of you would like to make the wish?"

"Nonsense!" declared the Mungling. "The Stone Tamer led *you* to the Dream Butter! It has to be you who makes the wish."

Reluctantly, quietly, Tabetha said, "I know." Then she exhaled in acceptance. "I know," she said again. She extended her hands for the bowl.

The wizard placed it into the cup of her joined palms, and without another thought she lifted the golden rim to her lips and tilted it. Creamy, warm liquid slipped down her throat. Electric sensations skipped up her spine. She handed the bowl back. She peered into the distance. Then she saw it. There, out in the desert beyond, waves of heat shimmered off the backs of the red dunes. Tabetha blinked as the sweat stung her eyes. She brushed it away.

Was her vision playing tricks?

"A city!" gurgled the Mungling around a mouthful of Dream Butter. He swallowed hard, shaking his head in disbelief. "A whole city is taking shape in the sand!"

Answer drank next, but already Tabetha felt as though she had snapped from a trance. Her vision had never been clearer. An entire city shimmered to life through the heat—great domes and towers and walls of red stone.

"The Lost City of Haza Mugad," breathed the boy-wizard. "We've unlocked it. The Dream Butter has unlocked the city!"

"Or awoken it," said Tabetha, even before she knew what she was saying. "Like something sleeping is now finally awake."

"Either way," he replied. "It's where the map has been hidden all these years. And whether awake or unlocked, it appears open to all, which means Morlac will be right behind. Quickly now!"

Answer started down the hill, toward the sparkling red towers. The Mungling galloped after him with Tabetha clutching his reins. The Lost City quivered like a mirage. Tabetha smelled the spice of red sand, of strange incense ahead. The sun-wyrm chattered on about the advice of mother Munglings and such, but Tabetha heard only the beating of her heart. It grew louder with each of his steps.

The Lost City beckoned like a hand.

♪

The Mungling halted before the gates of the Lost City, where massive walls rose high and red. Tabetha chewed her lip as she gazed upon the great entrance arch hanging above their heads. Her skin felt cool in its shadow, but her face burned, and she could hear the blood rampaging through her ears.

"Well, no point in waiting!" chirped the Mungling, knowing nothing of Tabetha's fear. He stepped toward the gate and then paused abruptly as the boy-wizard raised a hand. Answer turned his back to the gates, searching the desert dunes from which they had come.

"Do you see something?" Tabetha swallowed, the sour taste of dread on her tongue. "Has Morlac already caught up?"

Answer shook his head. "Something else," he said. "It's very strange, I admit, but . . ."

"What is it?"

The boy-wizard refused to explain. "You need not worry" was all he said. "I'll wait here, at the gate. You and the Mungling go in without me."

"No!" said Tabetha. "Not again. I won't leave you again."

The wizard took her hand. "Tabetha, listen to me. This is *your* journey."

"I know, but I still need your help."

"Shhh," he whispered gently. "Just listen, please." He brought a finger to his lips, and his eyes turned thoughtful and sad.

"If you saw in yourself," he began, "what I see now, you would understand why it must be this way. You would know why it is I, even with my sorcerous gifts, who look to you for all hope."

"That makes no sense," she said. "You're the most powerful person I know. If it weren't for you, I would never have come this far."

"If it weren't for you, Tabetha, Wrush would still be doomed," he said. "Don't you see? There's something about you, the way you are, the way you do things. It's *you* who are meant to find the Beginning Well. Not me. It's *you* who must ask the Luck

Fish for the Pyramid Map, and *you* who must bring it safely from Morlac's grasp."

"I still don't understand. Why can't you come too?"

"You will always be my empress, Tabetha, as I am forever your wizard. Your duty is to protect the people, but mine is to protect you, and that is best done from right here, at the gates of this city. You'll understand soon, I promise." He gave her a wink and something of that mischievous grin, only this time it seemed sad, too.

"Now go."

Tabetha forced back the tears, remembering the last time they'd parted. He was right, though, and she had to be brave. "Come on, Tabetha," the Mungling said kindly. He reached up to pat her foot. "The Luck Fish is somewhere within this Lost City, and if anyone is worthy of a wish, it's you." Tabetha said nothing, looking up at the gates. Her fear of wishes, she decided, was hers alone. There was no need to burden others with her worries. She took up the Mungling's reins, and together they passed beneath the immense arch of the Lost City.

Then they halted with a sudden gasp.

The sky shut black.

The gates slipped away.

Stars flooded the heavens, and Tabetha heard a magical hiss. The walls and ceiling of the city blurred with strange movement, and Tabetha twisted in place, peering behind her. The entrance she had come through was nowhere to be seen.

"A maze," whispered the Mungling.

Tabetha's breath came sharp. She began panting with fright. She heard another hiss, and the walls shifted again. *It's alive*, she thought, searching the cunning red walls of the labyrinth. *The walls of this place are as alive as snakes.*

Each block was fashioned from sparkling red stone—tremendous, immovable, impossibly heavy. Yet every few moments, a hiss sang through the air and Tabetha's vision would swim as the walls shifted like desert dunes.

"This way," Tabetha pointed, trying to keep her voice from trembling. She really had no idea where to go. She only knew they had to hurry.

The Mungling started down a hallway, then stopped abruptly at a hiss. The walls became a blur. Tabetha held tightly to her saddle, watching the maze smear and reshape like swift clouds in the wind. When the paths resumed, Tabetha found not one but two hallways before her. The maze had split into different directions.

"Which way now?" asked the Mungling.

Tabetha felt a knot in her belly. Her hands pressed nervously together. "I don't know."

Her eyes went anxiously to the walls, to the stones arching overhead, then paused. "But wait. There's something here." She leaned closer. "They're like letters. Or words." Tabetha brought her fingers up to touch them, carved as they were, into the stones beside the entrance to a hall.

"Does it say which way to go?" asked the Mungling.

"No," Tabetha replied, her fingertips tracing out the letters. For a brief moment, she was reminded of the raindrops outside her hospital window, how she had traced them with her fingers, imagining the droplets in a race. But there had been no race. Nor had her raindrop gone where she had expected. In the end, it had followed another path altogether.

"No," Tabetha repeated. "These letters don't tell us where to go. I think . . ." She paused in disbelief. "I think they tell a story."

"A story?" The Mungling wrinkled his puffy face in confusion.

Tabetha nodded. "They tell the story of our arrival here. This is *our* story, Mungling. See here?" And Tabetha read aloud:

"*. . . then they said farewell to their wizard, and the young girl fell sad. She and her Mungling entered the city of Haza Mugad. And it was here the stars fanned the heavens and the walls took on a mischief of their own.*"

"But that only just happened!" blurted the Mungling. "That's impossible! What kind of story starts at the end?"

Tabetha shrugged. "It's what the letters say."

The Mungling looked suspicious until they noticed letters engraved beside the second hall, too. Tabetha read them. These letters told a different kind of story. It was not one of times past but of times yet to come, of people and places yet born.

"It's this way, Tabetha. It must be," he said. "Surely we're meant to see things of the future, for where else could your fortune lie?"

Tabetha thought for a while before shaking her head. "I don't think so, Mungling. Don't ask me why, but for some reason I think the first hall is ours. It's the first hall that holds any chance of our map being there."

"Very well," agreed the Mungling, ever happy to please her. He led them down the first hall, which had spoken of their arrival, but moments later the walls shifted again. All was a blur, and then two more hallways opened up before them.

"What do the letters say this time?" the Mungling asked. He pointed to the writing above one hall.

The lighting was poor, so he glowed brighter for Tabetha. "This one says '. . . *and they climbed the slopes of the ridge, upon which they found a wide wooden bowl. In it was the Butter of Dreams. So they drank deep of its wonders, and many strange—*'"

"That happened before," interrupted the Mungling. "We drank the Dream Butter *before* we said farewell to Answer and entered the Lost City."

"I guess the story of this hall moves backward, just as the other goes forward," said Tabetha. She agreed it was odd. "But backward or not, I'm even more certain than before. This is definitely the right way, Mungling. It has to be."

The Mungling chirped and muttered in consent. He carried her down the passages she chose. Each time the walls shifted, two halls would appear. Tabetha would read the writing aloud, and the Mungling hustled her down each long corridor, backward through time, telling the story of their adventures in reverse. They read of the Lightning Field and the Wink Hole, then of the Stone Tamer's satchel and the Ember Moths. They read of their climb down the rope ladder and of Etherios floating in the sky.

Soon the story surpassed them. It told of times long ago, before Tabetha was even born. It told of other people, distant places, distant ages, long-dead kings. The halls of Haza Mugad carried them backward to when all worlds were fresh and there wasn't yet anyone to name them. And still, Tabetha and the Mungling traveled on.

"And what does this one say?"

Tabetha read aloud of when the first tree was born, and then of the very first rock and cloud.

"How about this one?"

She read of an age before stars, of when possibility ruled without light to mark one place from another.

"And this?"

Tabetha and Mungling halted, at last, before a hallway much larger than the others.

"Haza Mugad," Tabetha read aloud. "That's all this hallway says. *Haza Mugad.*"

"Haza Mugad?" repeated the Mungling, clearly expecting much more after his tour of the universe and its history. "But what does it mean?"

To Tabetha's surprise, she knew. Whether from the fragments of her dreams or the timeless magic of these halls, Tabetha couldn't quite say. But this much was certain: The story they followed, the story of the universe, had taken them backward through time until at last they'd reached the very ...

"Beginning," Tabetha whispered with wonder. "Haza Mugad means the *Well of Beginning.*"

"But there are no endings, Tabetha. Only beginnings in disguise."

o this is it!" chirped the Mungling, glowing yellow with the thrill. He pointed down the great corridor on their left. "Somewhere down this last hall is the Beginning Well, Tabetha, and in it the Luck Fish who can grant your wish. The Pyramid Map is as good as yours!"

Tabetha said nothing; in fact, she struggled to breathe. The word *wish* had by now grown so ominous in her mind as to make Tabetha tremble just to hear it. She urged the Mungling forward, her pulse hammering in her ears. But just as he crossed the threshold, the corridor dissolved like snowflakes at a touch. The floor was replaced by turquoise.

The enchanted lagoon.

Tabetha gaped at its beauty, at once haunting and bright. Beneath a night sky, the lagoon was somehow lit from within, as if the water itself was liquid blue light. Twinkling points of stars reflected across the calm of its surface, and seven glass towers bloomed from its depths.

In the center of the lagoon Tabetha spied the island. It was just as she recalled—a grassy mound pushing up through eerie blue waters, housing the topmost portion of a stone well.

"The wishing well," Tabetha said under her breath. Against the dark sky, it stood illuminated in her vision, almost too vivid for her eyes to behold.

"*The Beginning Well*," the Mungling corrected her. "And look here! The boat to it couldn't be more handy!"

The shore of the lagoon was laid with perfect glass bricks. Tied to them were seven glass boats. Each was shaped like a transparent bowl. The Mungling set Tabetha within one of the boats, kicked off from the bricks, and leaped down beside her.

"Look," Tabetha said, dragging a hand through the thick water. "Neither the boat nor my hand leaves the slightest ripple."

"Magical stuff, this water. Enchanted from top to bottom, I'd guess." The Mungling had taken up a single glass oar and now chattered to himself while paddling along. Tabetha listened, absorbed in the wonder of this place but unable to entirely forget what was to come.

I'm sorry, Tab, but no wish is worth more than a penny.

She felt a nervousness that made it hard to think.

She startled as the boat bumped up against the island shore. The Mungling clambered out and tied the boat in place. "The Luck Fish awaits you," he said with a deep bow, then leaned down to help Tabetha resaddle.

She couldn't help it. She had to ask. "Mungling," she said as he carried her out onto the island grass, which shone violet in the starlight. "Mungling, do you ever worry I might lead you wrong?"

"Never," he replied without pause, climbing the small mound toward the well.

"But what if I don't find the Pyramid Map? What if the Luck Fish won't give it to me?"

"Then you'll find another way. You always do."

Tabetha looked down at her hands. They shook. "I just don't want to disappoint you. I don't want you to get all your hopes up. In case I fail."

The Mungling stopped. He looked at her.

"I doubt there is a single fear," he said, as if reading her thoughts, "that you couldn't leave behind if you tried. I know you, Tabetha. I've seen you do it before. You make it look easy as . . ." He halted. The Beginning Well and its weave of white bricks were now before them. "Easy as tossing pennies in a well."

L

After so many hard-traveled miles and unexpected turns, it seemed Tabetha Bright had finally reached her destination. This was it. She was here at last. So it might not surprise you, dear reader, to know that she was, despite all her fears and apprehension, overcome with a sudden feeling of *elation*. A word meaning, "So happy it hurts."

Indeed, *elation*.

Say it once and you will become a fan. It is a word like velvet on the tongue. A delicious word. A word so rich and creamy it can be spread across toast. And yet a word, I might add, used mostly by adults, but found chiefly in the hearts of children.

Yes, Tabetha was elated. Joy ran freely through the meadows of her mind, skipped merrily down the bumps of her spine. Until of course it crashed, as so many joys do, headlong into the brick walls of worry.

It's amazing how fast one mood replaces another. In a breath, Tabetha's belly resumed its churning like laundry and her pulse took on a nervous flutter. The well was directly before her. Slowly, she reached out and touched it once, as though testing its safety or poking a ghost, then stretched up high in her saddle for the rim. It was tall, this well. The Mungling pressed against the white bricks of its side, arching his back so Tabetha could reach higher still.

A wooden bucket rested atop the well's rim. Tabetha nudged it aside with the tips of her fingers, then grabbed hold of the well's edge. She pulled with all her might. Her fingers ached with the strain, and her legs dangled useless and heavy. The effort had her panting through her teeth. It was awkward and difficult, but Tabetha managed to sit herself atop the rim. She grabbed her legs at the ankle, and with a final grunt, swung them over the rim where they drooped inside the well like loose doll's limbs.

She rested for a while, much aware of the tightness in her chest, occasionally glancing down into the shaft of the well. Somehow, perhaps with the excitement of adventure, Tabetha had been able to forget her pneumonia for a time. It had been as though she were under a spell or inside a bubble of good health. A bubble, she now realized, that was slowly coming apart. As her fatigue caught up, her limbs felt thick and she found herself thinking suddenly of her bed. More disturbing was the heavy feeling that her illness, from here on out, would only get harder to ignore.

After catching her breath, Tabetha leaned down for a good look into the well. Her hair fell forward across her face. "Ooooh," she cooed into its depths. "It's so beautiful," and her voice echoed back with haunting clarity.

"What is it? What do you see?"

Tabetha turned back to the Mungling on the grass.

"The lagoon water," she said. "That same blue stuff. The bottom of the well is filled with it, and glowing like a lightbulb."

"Spectacular! And the Luck Fish?"

Tabetha peered closer. It was hard to see anything through the blue. She tucked a lock of hair behind her ear.

"I'll have to try and catch it," she said, and grabbed hold of the bucket. She lowered it into the well by its rope. It slapped against the liquid with a pleasant splash, but when she hauled the bucket back up, there was no fish within. Nothing but liquid blue light.

She dumped it out and tried again. And once more the bucket returned empty, with no sign of the white fish she sought. Down and then up again, Tabetha dipped the bucket into the well, thinking each time that it would be different. And fearing the same.

What *would* she do when the Luck Fish appeared? Would she even have the courage to speak? Memories of disappointment ran wild through her mind, followed by images of her friends in tears. She was setting herself up for disaster. *This is a mistake,* she thought, and yet she could imagine no way around it.

"Did you find the Luck Fish yet?" she heard the Mungling call as she frowned into the bucket for the hundredth time. She tipped the liquid out. "No," she said.

Something was wrong. She was missing something. Something crucial. Tabetha set the bucket down, wondering just how one is meant to catch a lucky fish anyway. It seemed an impossible task, now that she thought about it.

And it was at that very moment she became aware of a fist in her chest. Not a real fist, of course, but a tightness all the same. That very tightness she had experienced with the Stone Tamer. This, she realized, was her fear. This fist was all the disappointment she had ever hoped to keep out, all the wishes she had ever regretted.

And she let go. Just like that, she relaxed all at once. Aware of that fist, she felt one finger peel back. Then a second, and a third, and a fourth. As her fear of failure dissolved, her fear of disappointing others, she felt not a fist but a hand, open and new, and a fresh wind blew all through her mind.

Perhaps it was no coincidence, but it was exactly then, as Tabetha peered through newly opened eyes, that she saw something glimmer in the well. It was the fish. She was certain. It had been there all along, just waiting, like Old Man Shale on the hill, for Tabetha to open up and let go.

No one can ever catch a lucky fish, she realized with a smile, *or else it wouldn't be lucky.* So Tabetha determined to set it free.

"Take the bucket," she said, handing it down to the Mungling. "Fill it with water from the lagoon and bring it back to me, fast as you can."

This he did, and after Tabetha dumped the water into the well she bid him do it again. Over and over, she poured lagoon water into the well and the level rose higher with each bucketful. Before long, her slippered feet dangled in the runny blue light. She added bucket after bucket until the fluid overflowed and rolled down the outside of the well.

The time had come. Tabetha set the bucket beside her. She took a deep breath and then leaned down close, her little fingers breaking the surface of the water. Then she gasped, straightening in surprise.

The loveliest fish, white as bone, chose that moment to leap from the blue.

As you know, Tabetha had seen a Luck Fish only once before, when she had journeyed through the Stone Tamer's magic satchel. Yet the fish's smiling little face and silky fins greeted her like something she'd known all her life. It jumped twice more, arching through warm night air, then dove gracefully as rain back into the liquid. When at last it wiggled to the surface, Tabetha held out her hand and the Luck Fish rested its chin upon her pale finger.

"Oh, little Tabetha," came the fish's clear voice. "At last you have come to me. I hope your journey here was kind."

"I enjoyed it very much," said Tabetha, who thought the iridescence of the fish's scales glittered like fresh snow under moonlight. "Parts were troublesome, I admit, but the sight of you now makes every step worth it."

"I see." The Luck Fish withdrew from Tabetha's hand, disappeared into the blue, and playfully resurfaced on the other side of her fingers. "Yet you do not try to catch me."

"Oh, no. I won't try to catch you, not now. I wish to set you free."

The Luck Fish peeked over the well's rim, studying the lagoon beyond. She met Tabetha's gaze. "That is your wish, then?" the Luck Fish asked. "To set me free?"

Tabetha hesitated. But it was not fear, this time, that held her back. It was that the Luck Fish granted only one wish to each visitor, and Tabetha needed her wish for something else. When she gazed upon the fish and considered the tragedy of such a wonder trapped for eternity in a well, she became sad.

"I'm not sure," she confessed. "I came a very long way to see you, but this isn't really the ending I had imagined."

"Ending?" the Luck Fish repeated, then paddled to the far side of the well.

"But there are no endings, Tabetha. Only beginnings in disguise." The fish dove, her last words hanging in the air. "Now come to me."

And with all the spirit of a girl who has leapt into bottomless holes, Tabetha pushed off from the well's brick rim. She felt the warmth of liquid light slip over her eyes as she sank toward the bottom of the Beginning.

Tabetha sank down and down until the well's bricks were no more, and the liquid light spread vast as an ocean. She breathed it in like fresh air. Her hands sliced through the fluid and left trails that lit up and then faded back into brilliant turquoise. Though she couldn't explain it, Tabetha sensed anything was possible in a place such as this. A place that was forever Beginning.

"You see?" said the Luck Fish, darting circles about her. "A beginning has no end. Here all things are possible. You need not free one who is already free. Now tell me once more, and think good and hard. What is your greatest wish?"

So Tabetha thought. Good and hard.

She was surprised to discover herself unprepared for this moment, as though she had never truly expected it to arrive. All along she had feared wishing and getting nothing at all. So she had wished for nothing, and now it seemed she could have anything in the world she chose. She found this just a little overwhelming.

Overwhelming? you reply. *Can I have her problem too? If only everyone had burdens such as this!* I can see your mind, dear reader, your imagination running wild. Even as you read this, your thoughts drift from the page.

So what *would* you do? What would you do with one wish?

Indeed, it's a question to make a person go mad. For Tabetha, there was the map, of course, which she had come all this way to retrieve, but there was also a heart-thumping surge of excitement. *Anything* was possible. All was in reach. With a wish came a broadening of view. It seemed suddenly wise to take pause for a moment, to consider options she might have overlooked. Certainly there could be no harm in this.

Just as you might, she went through lists in her head. She thought of all the things she had ever desired. She could wish to walk again, she realized, to sprint through the grass. She could wish to be healthy and happy and free.

Or, considering the task at hand, she could simply wish for Morlac's destruction, a whole universe in peace, or incredible powers all her own.

But had Tabetha wished for any of these things, it would be a different story I tell you now. A story that does not unfold as it should. For you will remember, dear reader, I made you a promise in Part One. I assured you of an event that would change the world! And it will—oh, it will—but not till the end of this tale, and only because Tabetha made each choice as she did.

So though she sifted through options, they passed like water through her hands. She could not hold them no matter how she tried. She sensed there was one wish, a right wish, and it was up to her to wish it. If only she just *knew* which wish it was.

And Tabetha froze. *That's it!* she realized. Her wizard's words floated through her mind.

Knowing is that voice, the one you thought you couldn't hear . . .

And it was the voice Tabetha could hear right now. "I wish," she said, a rush of certainty flooding through her veins, "I wish for the Pyramid Map. It's what I've known all along."

"Are you sure?" asked the Luck Fish. "You could wish for the pyramids themselves and save yourself all the trouble. You could even wish for your enemy in chains."

"Nope," said Tabetha. "It may not make sense, but I *know* this is the right decision. It's the Pyramid Map I wish for."

Without another word, the Luck Fish disappeared, a white streak darting back up to the well. Tabetha followed. When she broke through the surface and took her first breath of real air, she was surprised to find the Mungling balanced atop the white-brick rim of the well. His face was the picture of joy.

"Tabetha!" he exclaimed. "You've done it!"

She wrinkled her nose, wiping the blue liquid from her eyes. "Done what?"

"The Pyramid Map! You've found it!"

Tabetha saw nothing of the kind. "Where?" she asked, floating in the center of the well. "How do you mean?"

The Mungling simply pointed back at her. "There!" he called. "You're floating in the middle of it!"

Tabetha grabbed the Mungling's hand, and he pulled her up alongside him. The white bricks of the well's rim were still slick from the overflow, but the Mungling steadied her with four arms. She gazed back into the well, utterly astonished at what she saw.

The surface of the liquid was now lit with strange lines. Words were written there, too. As well as mountains. And cities.

And pyramids.

The map Tabetha sought now floated before her, a perfect diagram drawn with lines of illumination.

"Quickly!" she cried, pulling the magic pen from the small box in her pocket. "We have to make a copy before it disappears!"

The Mungling snatched a sheet of paper from his saddlebag. He gave it to Tabetha and then turned from her, offering the back of his head for her to write upon. Tabetha pressed the paper against him and began to copy what she saw in the well. The Mungling's skin was puffy and soft as a caterpillar's, which made drawing difficult in places, yet she managed in the end. So soon as she finished sketching the last city, labeling it with a name she could barely pronounce, the Luck Fish reemerged in the center of the well. Her appearance sent ripples through the fluid, breaking up the map like dazzling puzzle pieces.

"One last thing," said the Luck Fish to Tabetha. "Should you lose this Map, I can give you no other. But do not fear. The same shall be true for him."

"Him?" Tabetha asked. "For him who?"

"Me," came a voice, barely three steps behind. Tabetha gasped, turning. She clutched the map tight to her chest. Sitting atop a giant black Hinji, one hand clutching the matted hair of its neck, the helmeted rider gave a horrible laugh. "That's right, Tabetha. Me . . ."

Tabetha cringed, for as you may have guessed, reader, she was finally face to face with her most dreaded foe. His name escaped from her lips in a whisper.

"Morlac!"

"I pray you will forgive a loyal captain of Wrush!"

The evil sorcerer chuckled softly to himself, and Tabetha felt fear crawling like bugs beneath her skin. She stared, unable to move, as two hulking Gwybies came to stand at his side.

Two of them, she thought. *He's only brought two of his monsters.* She wondered if she and the Mungling could make it to the boat before they caught her. Then Morlac shifted in his Hinji's saddle, his black cape glistening smooth as water, and Tabetha saw what lay beyond him.

Forget that idea, she thought. Across the glowing blue waters of the lagoon, blurring the far shore with hair and fangs, was a whole army of Gwybies, pacing and leaping. Their horns twisted, scaly and sharp, under the light of the stars. Their howls made her blood run cold.

"It appears," said Morlac, his voice strangely familiar through the iron of his helmet, "that the Empress of Wrush is without her wizard. Has your Answer deserted you so soon?"

The Mungling leaped between them. "Stay back, Morlac!" he warned, his skin flashing bright as fire. "Her wizard may be gone, but she's not alone!"

At that, the evil sorcerer cracked the air with his laughter. His giant hyena snarled, and Gwybies gnashed their long teeth. "Not alone?" cackled Morlac. He glanced from one hideous Gwybie to the next. "I'm sure my pets here can fix that. It won't take more than a moment, I guarantee. And I wonder what you'll say then, Tabetha, after you've watched my Gwybies feast on your friend. Do you think you'll speak as bravely as he does now? I wonder. Do you think you'll have what it takes to face a dark sorcerer alone, knowing you are doomed to fail?"

Morlac snapped his fingers, and the two creatures at his side started forward. Tabetha saw their long, ratlike tails slap at the grass, and their foul reek hit her like a wave. Her stomach roiled. She wanted to be sick. Nonetheless, she sat without trembling, never turning from their awful eyes. It was just her and the Mungling, with no sign of help on the way. In a matter of moments, the map she had worked so hard to find would be gone, taken by Morlac. The situation appeared hopeless.

"But I'm not," she said aloud, for things were not at all as they seemed. It had happened quickly, and she'd had barely a glimpse at that, but when Morlac had snapped his fingers, Tabetha had seen something that gave her hope.

"Your creatures can't have my map," she announced to the black sorcerer. "Never. I found it, and it belongs to the goodfolk of Wrush."

"Then I will take it myself!" the sorcerer sneered, urging his Hinji forward.

"You don't need to," said Tabetha. "Because I plan to give it to *you*, Morlac, personally."

Morlac halted his Hinji in surprise. "Oh?"

"On one condition," she added.

"Tabetha!" whispered the Mungling anxiously. "What are you doing?" For like you, reader, the Mungling was surprised by her words. He had never dreamed she would give the map over to Morlac. But as I have already made clear, and as you have already seen, Tabetha was a very clever young girl.

"One condition," she repeated, "and it's yours, Morlac."

"One condition, you say?" Amused, Morlac threw a forearm across the front of his saddle and leaned forward. "This should be interesting, seeing as how you're on an island surrounded by my Gwybies. But I admit, I'm curious. Speak then, Empress. Name your condition."

"You must ask nicely," said Tabetha. "And hold out your hand the way anyone else would to receive a gift."

He didn't hesitate. Two steps of his Hinji and Morlac was before her, his face unreadable through the black slit of his helmet. He snorted to himself. "*May I?*" he chuckled, then stretched out his open hand.

And she grabbed it. "There!" she cried, turning the hand over in her own. "There, I knew it!" For just above Morlac's thumb, unmistakable as day, was a birthmark.

Shaped just like a sun.

Tabetha smiled as Thomas Morlac—her sullen hospital roommate—jerked his hand back, rubbing the birthmark with the other. "It makes no difference," the boy-sorcerer said, lifting the helmet's visor. "You still can't stop me."

Tabetha folded her arms. It all made sense now. She thought back to the pen she had seen Thomas writing with, day and night, the one that looked so much like her own. She thought back to the last words he had spoken to her, and how poorly he dealt with misfortune. So this was how he took out his anger! By creating an army of monsters and trying to take over the universe!

"Thomas," she said. "This isn't the way. You can't fix a problem by creating others. No matter how many worlds you conquer, you still won't be able to walk. You'll still be Thomas M., and I'll still be Tabetha, your hospital roommate. Using the map to find the Three Guardians won't change that."

"You're wrong!" he screeched.

"Tearing down the magic wall to Earth won't change that either."

Morlac breathed hard.

"Even if the Pump Dragons dig their tunnels, and your Gwybies follow them through, you'll still be a sad—"

"No!"

"—gloomy—"

"Never!"

"—miserable little boy in a wheelchair, hating the same world he controls."

Thomas M. went silent, his features rigid as wood. His eyes pinched closed, and Tabetha thought he might cry, but when they opened again she saw only anger. His face burned with it, red like flame.

"You don't even know me," he hissed, then snatched the Pyramid Map from Tabetha's hands. "You will, though, soon enough."

Morlac thrust the map into the air and the Gwybies howled like wolves at hunt. He wheeled his Hinji, and their excitement turned to shrieks. Tabetha saw them pacing and panting on the shore, reminding her of nothing so much as hungry animals in a cage.

"I don't like leaving the Empress of Wrush to such an awful end," he said. "But I'm afraid you leave me no choice, Tabetha. Besides, my Gwybies are famished after such a long march, and they could use a good meal before we search for the first pyramid." He started off on his Hinji, then said over his shoulder, "I hope my next roommate won't be so nosy."

"Hold, Morlac!" rose a voice from the far shore. "Your army is not the only one in Haza Mugad."

Tabetha's eyes strained through the dark, at last picking out the lone figure of another boy, this one standing alone but fearless in the gloom, his eyes bright as candles.

"Answer!" she cried, and then Tabetha's wizard stepped from the shadowy arches of the city, his tattoos glaring blue in the water's eerie light. The Gwybies turned as one to his voice, each taking a wary step backward.

"Quick, Tabetha!" the sun-wyrm whispered. "Get on my back! We'll sneak out now, while Morlac is distracted!"

"But the map," she said. "Thomas still has it!"

The Mungling shook his head. "There's nothing we can do."

Tabetha's hand dipped into her pocket, rattled small shells. "Nothing?" she said, hiding a small grin. She popped two Pepper Slugs into her mouth, and their spicy heat spread over her tongue as she quickly chewed.

"You are no army!" she heard Morlac call back to her wizard. "A sorcerer perhaps, but only one at that." He snorted angrily. "Gwybies! Bring the Low Wizard of Wrush to me!"

The Gwybies, however, never took that first step. Nor was Tabetha's boy-wizard alone for long. At that exact moment, the halls of Haza Mugad lit red with the glow of countless torches. The pounding echo of boots rang from the stone. Tabetha felt her pulse quicken as Isaac emerged, flickering torch in hand, leading an army of her own loyal soldiers from the Lost City's depths.

"Hooray!" she cheered, waving both hands in the air. The Gwybies snarled and howled. From atop the Mungling, she saw Isaac brandish his sword, and a thousand of his soldiers did the same. The Gwybies shrieked, clacking their long teeth in frustration.

"I'm sorry, My Lady!" Isaac shouted across the shore as he advanced on the stinking hordes. "But your words are contagious. I could not remain behind in Etherios when my own heart burned to follow. I pray you will forgive a loyal captain of Wrush!"

He slashed at the air and the Gwybies fell back. "I forgive you!" Tabetha shouted back with glee. "And more! Much more!"

Her skin trembled with joy. She smiled so wide, her cheeks ached. This must be why Answer had refused to enter the halls. He had seen Isaac approaching and remained behind at the gate, intending to lead Isaac and her army through the Lost City's maze.

"Gwybies!" cried Morlac, clapping down the visor of his helmet. "Retreat!" He spurred his Hinji to the island's shore, where his creatures tugged at the ropes holding his glass boat.

Tabetha's eyes went to the map in his hand. "Thomas," she said, her voice suddenly sad. "Don't do it. Please..."

Unexpectedly, he hesitated. Then he held up the map before him. "I've come too far for this, Tabetha. I ..." He shook his head, almost regretfully. "There's no turning back now."

Tabetha chewed fiercely, gathering the peppery spit on her tongue. "Then there's no going forward, either," she said. She pursed her lips, just as Answer had taught her. She cocked her tongue like a loaded weapon. She drew back her shoulders, arched her small back, sucked in a huge breath through her nose ...

And spat.

An enormous glob tumbled through the night air. It landed dead center on the map, carrying the blurred ink of names and places down the page as it slid to the bottom and dropped.

Morlac crinkled the ruined Map in his fist. "No!" he cried in a voice that shook the air, but Tabetha and the Mungling were already gone, slipping into their own glass boat and across the blue waters.

"I'll bet he never expected that from an empress!" laughed the Mungling as he worked the glass oar.

Tabetha turned, cupping her hands to her mouth. "I'll see you back home, Thomas!" she waved to him as he sat fuming on his black hyena. "But if you want cookies this time, you'll have to ask nicely!"

The Mungling waved too. "And hold out your hand, the way anyone else would!"

Tabetha and the Mungling escaped back through the twisting mazes of Haza Mugad while Answer, Isaac, and Tabetha's own army busied the monsters on the island shore. When at last she emerged into sunlight, the arch of the Lost City at her back, she gazed out onto the familiar red dunes. The light was dazzling, and she squinted into the glare, feeling exhaustion crash over her like a wave.

"Well, Mungling," she sighed, forcing herself upright in her saddle. "We almost did it. We almost got the Pyramid Map."

"At least the map won't do Morlac much good," said the sun-wyrm. "Not with your Pepper Slug spit all over it. That was some quick thinking on your part, Tabetha."

Tabetha patted his neck. "As usual, you were brave to the end. I only wish we had a copy of that map, too."

"You think Morlac can still use his?"

"It won't be perfect," she said. "Parts are blurred, but I think he'll still find the Three Guardians... eventually. I guess we'll just have to do our best to keep up." Tabetha patted the Mungling's neck again, looking down at him for the first time since leaving the city's darkness.

She frowned in confusion.

She leaned closer, her eyes nearly touching the puffy wrinkles at the back of his head.

"Mungling," she said, her voice suddenly breathless.

"Yes?"

"Mungling, you aren't going to believe this."

"What? What is it?"

Tabetha swallowed, straightening in her saddle. "There's a copy of the Pyramid Map right here, on the back of your head."

"What!" he cried. "Are you joking? Let me see!" He twisted his head one way, then cranked it the other, finally giving up with a huff. "Are you sure?" he asked at last.

"Don't worry," said Tabetha, chuckling in disbelief. "It's here. Right here, plain as day. The ink from my pen must have soaked through when I sketched the map against the back of your head."

"That means we can find the Three Guardians after all! We can keep Morlac from tearing down the Hedge!"

"What's more, our copy of the map is probably better than the blurred one he has."

"Yes, yes!" he chirped. "It also means—"

Bee-bee-bee-beep. Bee-bee-bee-beep.

Tabetha and the Mungling's eyes went to her wrist. Her watch alarm rang over and over again.

"Oh, no," she whispered. "The nurses will be coming any minute to give me my medicine! I have to be back before they come."

Her thoughts went to Thomas, who got his medicine at noon too. He would be racing back about now, just like her.

"Don't worry, Tabetha," said the Mungling reassuringly. "You go ahead. You need to. I'll wait here for Answer and Isaac."

She hesitated. "After all we've been through, I hate to leave him once more. It seems like each time I see Answer, I'm saying good-bye."

"He'll understand. He always does."

"And poor Isaac, too. He came all this way to help." She paused. "But most of all, I think I'll miss you, Mungling. I wish I could bring you with me."

The Mungling smiled sadly. "We both know that's not possible, Tabetha. Not until I find my name."

She sighed. "You be extra careful then, until I get back," she said. "*You* are the Pyramid Map now, Mungling, and if anything happens to you—"

"I get the idea." The Mungling brought a hand up to touch the markings behind his head. "I guess no more swimming for me then. Or baths."

She playfully swatted his hand away. "No more touching the back of your head, either. We don't want any of that ink to rub off."

He smiled. "Go on, Tabetha. We'll all be waiting for you in Etherios when you return."

With that, the Mungling handed Tabetha the last sheet of paper from his saddlebag. "I'd make a copy of the map right now," she said, "but I'll need this one to get back." Using the outer wall of the city this time, Tabetha pressed the paper flat and began to write. She wrote about her hospital room and the curtains pulled in a tight ring about her bed. She described her wheelchair, and the nurses, and the stuffed animals by her pillow. She even described the little orange pills they brought her each day at noon.

Last of all, she wrote about Thomas. She described him in his own bed, near the window, making sure the sunlight lit his face and warmed him. Strange as it seemed, she still wished Thomas well. She knew what it was to be lonely and sad, and to wish for running shoes on her feet instead of hospital slippers. Tabetha shared Thomas's sorrow. She shared his pain and his loss. But what did it take to share something more?

Tabetha wrote and she wrote. As she felt herself carried away by the pen's magic, and the colors of her room came slowly into focus, she found herself wondering what the quietest voice in Thomas's heart was like, and whether he might listen to it if she asked him to.

As if waking from sleep, Tabetha became aware of the softness of her sheets beneath her. The room's light was dim, slipping faintly through the crack where her curtains met at the foot of her bed. She realized she was back in the hospital. Tabetha pushed herself up in bed, glancing at the big clock on the wall. She still had a minute before the nurses would arrive.

She looked hesitantly at the closed curtain. Biting her lip, she leaned forward and clasped its rough edge. She took a deep breath.

She yanked it back.

Light poured through the window on the far side of the room, and she shielded her eyes with her arm. She blinked, momentarily blinded, as a blurry figure shifted before the sill. A boy on his bed, bathed in golden light. She inhaled sharply, just as he yanked his own curtain across the window, and in the darkness that followed she saw him clearly.

There, barely ten feet from her own bed, was Thomas Morlac. Not just a sorcerer, mind you, or an agent of evil—not just a dangerous enemy to all the known universe—but Tabetha's roommate.

With cookie crumbs on the floor by his slippers.

Coming Soon . . .

VOLUME TWO

Wrush: Tabetha's Last Task

The countdown has begun. In a race against Morlac and her own fading strength, Tabetha must return to Wrush and find the Three Guardians. But something's wrong with her pen, and Morlac has found a way to travel through time. Now with the help of a magic salamander, Tabetha and her friends must continue their journey between worlds, searching for a way to save Wrush from the dark sorcerer.

But will she find the pyramids before Morlac? Will the Hedge be destroyed? As time runs out, Tabetha is forced to reveal her greatest secret—one that nobody, not even her closest friends, would ever expect . . .

Want to get published?
Check out
Secret Worlds Magazine!

S*ecret Worlds* is a magazine just for kids, filled with stories and artwork created by readers like you. If you've ever wanted to publish a story or a poem, or see your artwork in print, then now is your chance. Just go to www.TheSecret-Worlds.com, click on *Secret Worlds Magazine*, and learn how you can share your creativity with the world!

And there's more ...

Secret Worlds is also where you can go to read secret letters from The Karakul, get updates on the book series, answer quizzes, read interviews, and get your fill of everything Tabetha Bright.

Acknowledgments

A word of thanks is owed to the many people who contributed to this book's creation. Among them are the following individuals, for whose help the author is especially grateful:

Alan Grimes, Allyn Gandall, Angela Baldinger, Anika Enfield, Astrid Bjorlo, Ayla Gandall, Betty Ann Gandall, Chris d'Lacy, Daniel Ruke, Dave Berezan, Dawn Bain, Debbie Hanzen, Dennis Willmott, Diana Harrison, Erik Hanzen, Fonda Spooner, Jaide Ashcroft, Jennifer Korchinski, John de Ruiter, Jonah Hanzen, Justin Branch, Leala Enfield, Linda Sloan, Lucille Charois, Marian Willmott, Mauve Lafleur, Pearl Mendel, Raigan Enfield, Susan Enfield, Terry Enfield, Travis Enfield, Trevor Reddekopp, the Writers' Federation of New Brunswick, and finally to *Crow Toes Quarterly* for publishing a chapter of the manuscript in their magazine.

About the Author

Little is known of him. His manuscripts were delivered to the publisher by riderless camel. Strange, cryptic instructions, or possibly threats, were included. His real name we do not know, but of karakul in general, the dictionary has this to say: "Karakul are a hearty species of sheep from the highland plateaus of Turkmenistan. Their wool was traditionally used in the production of Persian rugs." It is possible the author sees himself as a ram of sorts: hardheaded, gruff, and argumentative, but ultimately protective of his flock, having great affection for the least small lamb. We think he lives in a cave. Or maybe Canada.